GENTLEMEN PREFER BROOMSTICKS

ACCIDENTALLY MAGICAL AT MIDLIFE? BOOK THREE

MELINDA CHASE

GENTLEMEN PREFER BROOMSTICKS

When I said I wanted an adventure, maybe I should've been a bit clearer...

See, I imaged a *Harry Potter* or *Disney-style* adventure. You know, the kind that comes with plenty of fun, romance, and the promise of a happy ending.

Instead, my adventure is looking like something out of *Game of Thrones*.

My Shade-filled dreams have been replaced with a recurring nightmare, and there's a random Banshee seemingly haunting mine and Willa's house.

Just when I think nothing else could happen, Shade literally drops through my roof with not-so-good news.

The King Collector is here.

And it turns out, this time, he's coming for Willa and me…

Gentlemen Prefer Broomsticks *is the third book in the brand new series:* **Accidentally Magical at Midlife?** *from author Melinda Chase.*

Melinda loves writing tales that prove life—romance—and 'happily-ever-afters'—do exist beyond your twenties! Her books feature snarky, hilarious heroines and their wild adventures of mid-life self-discovery filled with mystery and romance. It's sure to please fans of traditional paranormal romance and cozy paranormal mysteries!

Callie

MY HAND SLIPPED across the smooth leather binding of one of Willa's yard sale finds before I set it into an empty slot on the bookshelf.

I used to think that she just liked old books, but from the way she feverishly looked through them every time she found a table full, I was starting to think it was her looking for some random piece of home someone thought was nothing more than a fairy tale book. After spending so much time in the Fae Realm, I was starting to feel that draw to it as well. I didn't think I would actually miss it there. Everything had been so stressful, but after being back for a couple of weeks, working like nothing had ever changed, the fear had become nothing more than a memory for me.

Sliding the last book in my hands on the back shelf, I stretched my arms over my head and dragged my feet as I slowly made my way toward the front of the Lustrous Bean. I loved our little coffee/book shop, but I was exhausted. I covered my mouth as I yawned, my eyes open just enough to ensure I didn't run into anyone, or trip over anything. I was attempting to spend the next couple of weeks injury free, which was a long shot considering my natural clumsiness, and the fact that twice I had been thrown into a wild crazy situation, but I still had hope.

"Tired?" Willa asked, standing bent over behind the checkout desk. She had both of her elbows propped on the countertop, and though I could see and now recognized the Fae radiating from her cheeks, she still looked more tired than usual.

I nodded my head, having a chain reaction of yawns. All that came out was a grunt.

Willa slowly shook her head and giggled. "Me too."

I leaned my hips into the counter and tapped my hands on the smooth surface. "Let me guess, it's the banshee."

Willa chuckled and shook her head. "That I can deal with. When I was growing up in the Fae castle, my room was right next to a troll's. He was one of the dignitaries. He snored so loud it sounded like deep horns shaking the walls. I've just been having strange dreams lately."

I tried to hide the chill that ran up my back. Dreams and I had a strange relationship. Before I went to the Fae Realm, my dreams were of Shade, topless, asking me to ride on his broomstick.

After I got back though, that all changed.

I had the same dream over and over again, and it made no sense at all. It was eerie, and I woke from it covered in sweat every single time. I had always been cautious, but I had turned into the girl that checked the closet and under her bed before she went to sleep at night. With everything going on though, I didn't want Willa to worry. I really didn't think it was anything more than my nightly bowl of Monkey Chunk ice cream sending weird sugar induced dreams into my night rest. But with Willa having strange dreams too...

"What about?" I asked, holding back a cringe

over asking a question I really didn't want to know the answer to.

She stared at me for a minute, tapping her fingers on the countertop. I wasn't sure what she was thinking, but I could tell that there was contemplation going on in that little Fae brain of hers. "I don't know, it's a weird dream. I keep having the same one over and over again."

I meant to just quietly swallow down the anxiety rising, but it came out as almost a cartoonish gulp. "That's weird..."

Willa didn't seem to notice my nervousness, which was odd because she always noticed everything about me.

She let out a deep breath and stood up straight, stretching her arms over her head. "I mean, it's not like weirder stuff doesn't happen to us. That being said, the dream doesn't make much sense at all. It's like I'm looking through someone else's eyes, but I can't figure out who I am. I know where I am, just not who I am."

I leaned forward a bit, curious if it had anything to do with my dream. Before Willa could continue though, the bells on the front door jingled and two tourists came walking in, laughing wildly. The woman was middle-aged, a visor holding her obviously bleached hair back, and a

T-shirt that said, "I love the beach." She cleared her throat and smiled at the two of us. "I know it's late and you're probably getting ready to close, but we just wanted to grab a couple of coffees before we headed back to the hotel."

I glanced over at Willa who put on the perfect smile and hopped to it, taking their orders. I slinked slowly away, my mind too full of dreams to hold some sort of fake conversation with people that I could care less about. They would be the last customers of the night, which was good. I wanted to go home. Willa and I had planned to cook dinner and nestle in for a movie before bed. She was still staying at my place, too worried about my safety to leave me alone. I had to admit, even with my talking cat and dog bantering non-stop, having Willa there made me feel a lot less alone.

By the time the tourists left, I had already straightened up the rest the place and any talk of dreams had gone to the back burner. Willa locked the door after they left and turned and smiled at me. "You know what I've been thinking about all day?"

"What? The meaning of life? The next book you'll buy?"

She giggled. "No, I've been thinking about the

coffee in the Fae realm. They have the best coffee."

I rolled my eyes and groaned. "I know. It was on my list to bring it back here so that we could become billionaires, but I forgot all about it. It's really good, but those tarts that were at the party..." My lips pursed, realizing that Callie hadn't really been awake for the party, or ball as they called it.

She chuckled as she walked over to the swinging door, reached into the back room, and flipped off the light switch. "I don't really remember it from that night, but I definitely have had those a million times. They were my favorite. The ones with the berry custard filling... My father brought those to my birthday every single year when I was little."

We continued closing up the shop, and though Willa was really good at hiding her feelings, I could tell there was a bit of sadness in her tone when she talked about her father.

How could there not be?

She hadn't seen him in many years and on top of that, he was missing. Whether the King Collector and his gang of brooding caped creatures took him or not, we still didn't know. But we did know that it wasn't that he had just run off for vacation. Something nefarious happened, and though we didn't really talk about it much, there'd been a lingering nervousness in the pit of my stomach ever since we returned from the Fae realm.

Of course, that could be my dreams, or even the banshee that wouldn't shut up.

Either way, he was still missing and I knew that eventually we were going to have to start looking for him again.

We left the shop and Willa locked up before we jumped in her car and headed to the house. As we drove, I squinted my eyes, looking out at the barely visible ocean waves sparkling beneath the crescent moon. Far in the distance I could see the hill that my parents were buried on, but it no longer made me incredibly sad to see it. Maybe it was just that my body was so tired from emotions that I didn't have anything left. But I also hoped that it was because I was getting stronger and those feelings of loss after all those years had finally started to turn into good memories of when they were alive.

Turning back to Willa, I studied her for a moment, watching as her eyes stared forward through the windshield, but her attention was obviously somewhere else. "Do you miss it?"

She lifted her eyebrows but didn't look at me. "What's that?"

I shrugged. "The Fae realm. I'm sure after being here for all these years it was easy to be away because this is your home, but going back I'm sure brought up a lot of old memories."

A smile pulled at her lips. "I do. I especially miss it now that my uncle is in charge and things are starting to settle down there. I miss the holidays that we had, and all the decorations and happiness. But there are a lot of things that I don't miss. I have to admit though, after seeing the sunset and skylines of the Fae realm, things aren't quite as beautiful here anymore. I'm sure that'll fade away again."

"Does it have to?" I clasped my hands in my lap, not sure whether I was stepping over the line or not. "I mean, after we find your father…"

"If," Willa said, cutting me off. "If we find my father."

My brow furled and I turned toward her shaking my head. "Don't say that. Of course we're going to find him. People don't just take people and never pop up somewhere. They always have a reason for it. And when your father's a king… Why would someone just take him and never return him?"

Willa glanced over at me and then back at the road as we pulled down the drive toward the house. "I know you're starting to understand this, but you have to remember that the creatures in other realms are not like us here. While they like things just like humans, they don't covet money over everything else. There are a million reasons why someone would take the king and... Well, get rid of them. But I haven't given up hope if that's what you think. I just want to be realistic with myself. You know, I don't want to get myself all riled up thinking that I'm going to find him at any moment and then I don't. It would be heart-breaking to say the least."

I sighed and turned back in my chair, knowing full well that she was right. I had lived my life that way since my parents had died. I liked being realistic about everything so that there was no chance that I'd be unprepared for an outcome. I just wasn't used to Willa living that way. She had always been so optimistic about everything, and I didn't want that to change about her.

When we pulled up to the house and put the car in park, Willa just sat there staring at the front door. I followed her gaze up, finding a small fluttering and glowing orb hovering halfway up the door. I lifted a brow. "Uh, is that a cousin of yours?"

She rolled her eyes and stared at me, shaking her head. "I thought you understood that Fae are not fairies. Besides, that's not a fairy, that's just an orb of magic. I'm actually surprised you can see it because there's definitely a cloaking spell on it."

When she said that, the bracelet on my wrist tingled. I held up my arm and shrugged. "I've got the magic touch apparently. But if it's not a creature, and is just a ball of magic, where's it from and what does it want?"

Willa reached for the door handle. "I can sense Fae magic, so I'm assuming it's some sort of message from home. Come on, let's check it out."

As she got out of the car, I mumbled to myself, opening my door as well. "Oh sure, everything we do turns out to be some sort of crazy adventure somewhere. Let's just go see what the magical orb floating at the door wants."

As we approached the orb, it began to flutter toward Willa. She stopped and put her hands out. It floated over top of her palms and sat there for moment as if it were attempting to recognize her. After a few moments it settled against her skin and the outer orb evaporated, dropping a folded piece of paper in her hand. She looked at me and smiled. "See? I told you it was a letter."

She looked behind us and then grabbed the keys, pushing them into the door. "Let's get inside though. Who knows who could be lurking around here."

"Thanks. I wasn't nervous, but now I am."

She ignored me as we walked inside. Both Mr. Hobbles and Bean were curled up on the couch fast asleep. Mr. Hobbles opened his eyes, yawned, and then shut them again. At least he paid attention to who came in the house. Apparently though, floating orbs outside the door were beyond his feline senses.

Willa sat down on the other end of the couch and I took the chair next to her. She opened up the folded pieces of paper and I leaned forward, blinking. "It's blank."

She grinned wildly and pressed her thumb to the paper. A slow rolling wave of color washed over the paper and the strokes of a pen began to appear. My mouth dropped open. "No matter how many times I see it, this magic stuff will never get old. It's like living inside of a movie."

Willa threw her head back and laughed. "Living in this realm, I appreciate it too."

I rubbed my hands together anxiously. "What's it say? Who's it from?"

Clearing her throat, Willa sat up tall and began to read the letter out loud. "Dearest Niece, Princess Willa and Brave Callie, I hope that this letter finds you safe and comfortable in the human realm."

"It's from your uncle," I said with far too much excitement. It was like Christmas.

Willa nodded with the same enthusiasm and continued. "Alabaster and I have been busy fixing all the things that my sister had purposefully destroyed. There's a lot of neglect of the kingdom as you can probably imagine. We've heard no word from her or seen any sign of her since before you left. We have also taken the time to put together a task force whose sole purpose is to begin searching for your father, the King."

Willa glanced up at me and twisted her nose. "I've always wanted to be part of something like that. Now, I really do because it has to do with finding my father."

I reached out and patted her knee. "You'll have your chance. Don't let the quiet, or semi-quiet around here fool you."

She continued without a response. "We will let you know as soon as we have any leads. We are also in touch with the witches in case we see or hear any sign of the Witch King. We hope that you're staying safe in the human realm and I can't wait to see you again one day. If you need anything, you know how to get hold of us. With love and best regard, Your Uncle."

Below his signature was the Fae realm seal and it shimmered with magic before the writing faded away. I sat back in my chair and Willa leaned back against the couch. We were both so excited to read the letter, but now it felt almost as if it was a letdown. For a moment, we were back with our uncles, but as soon as it was done, we returned to the human realm where nothing was happening, we didn't really know what to do or where to look, and we lived in our memories. It was a helpless feeling, one I had felt after my parents' accident, and my idea of what to do wasn't any better then, either.

Willa let out a small sigh and sat up, placing the letter in her open palms. She whispered something and leaned very close, blowing on it. As her magical breath moved over the paper, it evaporated into a shimmering blue waterfall of magic, until it was completely gone. She clapped her hands together and a smile returned to her face. "Come on. Let's make our dinner and have our night of relaxation. There's nothing we can do at this point."

As soon as we both stood though, the low, deep tone of the banshee's song echoed out through the house. My body went rigid as it did every single time I heard it. "Oh yeah, for a second I had almost forgotten that death's buddy was sitting on our doorstep."

2

Callie

THE SOUND of sizzling shrimp echoed through the house as Willa dropped the prepared seafood into the frying pan.

The aromatic essence of sautéed shrimp, carefully prepared crab cakes, and roasting garlic Brussel sprouts permeated to all corners of the kitchen. Just seconds after the shrimp hit the pan, Mr. Hobbles and Bean came running into the room. Bean feverishly sniffed the floor looking for any sort of crumbs, and Mr. Hobbles jumped up on the countertop, sitting down on the edge as he inspected what we were doing. Both of them still looked tired, and neither of them said a word. I knew that would only last for a few minutes, but I was going to enjoy it while it lasted.

I sat at the island, snacking on small scraps of cooked crabmeat while Willa took care of dinner. We had our place in the kitchen and mine was nowhere near the stove. I did all the chopping and preparing and Willa did the cooking. She was a fantastic cook and I knew there was no magic involved. Between the numerous cooking classes she had taken over the years, the cooking shows she watched religiously, and the dozens of cookbooks she had acquired, she had become a chef in her own mind. It was a good thing, because if I was in charge, we would've been living off of take-out and pizza.

Willa glanced over her shoulder at me as she moved the shrimp around in the pan. "So, have any more of those hot, topless, broomstick aeronautic dreams about Shade?"

My shoulders stiffened and embarrassment ran through me. I had nearly forgotten that right after we got back from the Fae realm, and had more than a couple of bottles of wine between us to relax, I had told her about the dreams. I could tell she had been waiting patiently to bring it up again. I shook my head. "No. No more broom-stick dreams."

Willa chuckled, turning back to the stove. "I mean, I can't blame you. Those definitely sound better than me wandering around..."

Before she could finish her sentence, the timer went off for the Brussel sprouts and she opened up the oven, fanning the heat away. She glanced over at me with a smile. "Dinner is just about ready. Is the movie all set?"

I nodded, moving from the chair, my mind still on my dreams. "Yep, sitting there ready to press play. I'll get our plates down."

As I reached up into the cabinet, the banshee wailed again and I froze just like Willa did, cringing at the sound of it. When it had faded away, I grabbed the plates and set them heavily down on the countertop. I crossed my arms over my chest and turned around, irritation filling me. "We've been home for weeks. I thought for sure that something would happen with this woman, ghost lady, living in our house. She could at least have the common courtesy to come and talk to us."

Willa walked toward me with a tray of crab cakes and I moved out of the way as she filled our plates. "Banshees are complicated creatures.

Sometimes they're so caught up in their own instincts they don't think about the fact that we don't live in their world. They have a job and they're doing it, and usually they're propelled to do it by their own ancestral base needs. I would like to talk to her though."

"Maybe she's not here for you," the cat said, rather brusquely. "You aren't the only beings living in this house."

I raised my brow at him. "She's here for you? I think that's kind of presumptuous."

If a cat could roll his eyes, he would have. "No, human." He turned his head several times toward Bean, but didn't say anything.

"In your dreams," Willa replied.

Mr. Hobbles laid down on the counter and sighed. "Could I ever be that lucky?"

I shook my head. "I don't know. I have a sneaking suspicion that this isn't random. I personally don't think anyone is doomed to die. I think this has something to do with the King Collector, but without talking to her, I will never know. I do know that if she doesn't quiet down, I'm going to call a priest or something."

Willa shoved my plate into my hands and put a fork on it. "Banshees have nothing to do with religion. Religion is different in every realm. They aren't ghosts or poltergeists."

I followed Willa out into the living room and sat down on the couch next to her. With my plate sitting in my lap, and Bean at my feet waiting for me to drop even a crumb, I thought about the banshee. "Is she here or is she just projecting her spooky moans to our house?"

Willa picked up the remote and pressed pause. "I'm not sure. I can definitely feel her presence, but she could be poking out from another realm and then going back. I feel like if she were here, we would know it. This place isn't big, no offense, and like I said, she's not a ghost. She's a real person, flesh and blood."

I leaned back against the couch, and let Willa go ahead and play the movie. It wasn't very often that she got frustrated, but I could tell from her tone that she was holding back. She didn't want to talk about the banshee, she just wanted to relax. I wanted that too. Unfortunately, relaxing was really hard for me to do, especially sharing my house with so many different beings. I didn't want to ruin her relaxation though, so I pulled my legs up beside me, placed my plate on my lap, and enjoyed a home-cooked meal for once. The movie was a romantic comedy and Willa giggled and laughed the whole time. I had seen it about fifty times, and my mind was somewhere else, but I made sure to smile or laugh whenever she looked over at me.

I knew I wasn't fooling her, she could sense my anxiety no matter where she was, but at least she knew that I was trying for her. After the movie, I did the dishes while Willa vacuumed up the hair off the couch and made her bed for the night. I was starting to think that her sleeping at my place wasn't just for my comfort but for hers as well. She was basically living there, but without a bedroom. I had even given her half of my closet and half of my drawers so she could stop running back and forth to her house every morning to change clothes. Despite the lack of personal belongings, she did bring back all of her crafting supplies and they were strewn about on the coffee table where she sat most evenings gluing, and pasting, and cutting, and glittering to her heart's content.

I knew when it was an extra stressful day for Willa because she went hard on the glitter, and not only did my living room shimmer like diamonds, but in the right light, Bean glistened as well. The cat tended to stay away from the living room glitter pile after accidentally jumping up on the coffee table one day and spending the next four days licking glitter off of himself. He found it to be the crafting of the devil, or so he called it. Personally, I thought Mr. Hobbles looked a little bit kinder with tiny bits of sparkly confetti peppered throughout his fur.

Normally, after dinner we would have dessert and then sit around and talk until it was far too late and we either fell asleep on the couch or I stumbled off into my room and passed out on the bed. However, it was obvious that neither of us had been sleeping very well, so after dinner, it was really unsaid, but we both wandered off to our respective sleeping locations. The banshee had sung out several times during the movie but after it was done, she had quieted. I assumed she had gone to bed as well. She rarely sang out in the middle of the night anymore. It was probably because she got no response considering both Willa and I could sleep hard if we wanted to. And lately… I really wanted to.

Even after our attempts to adult our way to bed early that night, by the time I got under the covers and looked at my phone, it was close to midnight. I groaned inwardly as I switched off the light and clicked on the alarm. Another night of just five hours of sleep before we had to be at the shop the next morning. I was having a hard time balancing work, magical work, and personal time. By the time I was done working at the shop and trying to figure out the mysteries I had seen over the last couple of months, I dove headfirst into my personal time. Far too often I forgot to keep track of what time it was and landed in the same situation I was in at that moment.

Suffice it to say, it didn't take me very long to fall asleep that night. It also didn't take very long for the dreaded dream to come rushing back to me. Just like every other time I had it, I found myself in a damp and dark cave-like place. Ahead of me was a doorway, a natural one carved into the cave. I could feel the urge to rush forward, like I was looking for something. No matter how many times I told myself in my dream to not run forward, knowing full well what I was going to see on the other side of that doorway, my feet moved without my mind in control.

I hurried through the doorway hearing my name being called from behind and rushed straight through, coming to a brisk stop a few paces inside. Sprawled out in front of me was a large open landscape. Everything was a different shade of gray, and a dense fog rolled suspiciously across the ground. I turned back around toward the door, but it was gone. The landscape stretched out in all directions. Looking down at my feet, the fog inched closer. As it did, I realized it wasn't fog at all. Straining my eyes, I could make out faces and whispering bodies within the haze. What I thought was fog was actually ghosts, spirits, or whatever you wanted to call them. Their faces were stretched out and I could suddenly hear the whispering of thousands of voices all around me.

A feeling of dread crept over me as the sound of shuffling feet behind me brought the realization that beyond the ghosts, wherever I was, I wasn't the only living being. In fact, that was the precise moment in my dream every night when I woke up, and I kicked myself for waking up before I had a chance to figure out what was going on. But this time, it was going to be different. I had willed myself to turn around at that point in my dream so hard before I went to sleep there was no way, even in a dream state, I was going to forget.

I clenched my fists, trying to find my bravery, but as I turned my body, preparing myself for whatever was standing behind me, a loud crackling sound shook me and I froze solid with the spirits swirling around my feet. Almost directly after, a loud boom pulled me straight from my sleep and I sat up in bed, my eyes wide, listening as something crashed down outside of my room. Even my dog, normally soundproof and snoring, sat up with perked ears and a low grumble in his throat.

The illusion of safety was over, and I knew whatever was sitting outside of my room, crash landing there, wasn't accidental. Whoever it was, or whatever it was, had come for me or Willa and I hoped, as I pulled myself from the bed and slipped on my slippers, it hadn't already gotten Willa. We had made it that far, barely and by the skin of our teeth sometimes, but I wasn't about to be taken down by an unwanted houseguest. I was really tired of random beings impeding on my personal space. If they wanted to come to my house and start trouble, human or not, I would give it right back to them.

Whether I would survive it or not was a completely different story.

3

Callie

I RUSHED to the door and paused, Bean close behind with his fur standing straight up along his spine.

Glancing over, I thought about grabbing my trusty flat iron that still seemed to be the best weapon in the house, but then the bracelet on my wrist tingled and I remembered all the times that I had defended myself without even truly knowing what I was doing. I didn't need a flat iron anymore. I was starting to become more and more comfortable with the idea of magic flowing through me, even if it was temporary. The magic in the bracelet had seemed to save me every time and had an intuitive effect, changing the magic dependent upon what foe I was facing.

Whatever was on the other side of that door couldn't be much worse than what I had already faced, though my cat seemed not happy at all. Instead of human words, all I could hear were shrill shrieks of cat sounds followed by long hissing anger. Remembering that Willa was sleeping on the couch, I grabbed the door handle and flung open the door, racing out. When I turned the corner into the living room, I came to a sudden stop, causing my dog to run face first into my legs.

Standing on the back of the couch, Willa was breathing heavily, her hands out with her palms up, sparks of Fae magic trickling from them. I scanned the room and my hands fell to my sides. Above us, there was a hole in the ceiling, and lying flat on his back, on top of a collapsed coffee table and piles of crafting material, was Shade. He groaned, reaching his hand up to rub his forehead and when he pulled it back, he gritted his teeth at the small scraps of paper stuck to his palms.

"Are you okay?" I asked, a small hitch in my voice.

It was shocking to see Shade lying there on the ground. I was so used to him being smooth and confident in everything that he did. It was both comical and alarming at the same time. I had no idea what would have caused Shade to come plummeting through the roof, crushing the crafting masterpiece that Willa had been working on for weeks. His eyes shifted to me and then over to Willa who had scooted down onto the edge of the couch and plopped down with her legs pulled to her chest as she caught her breath.

He slowly picked himself up, his brow furled as he stared up at the hole in the ceiling. "I'll fix that."

Willa raised a brow. "At least you're not hard to find anymore."

He looked at her, confused for a moment, and then followed her eyes to the front of his black shirt. He groaned and threw his head back, rolling his eyes as he attempted to brush the glitter from the front of him. Willa snickered and shook her head. "It's no use. Even the strongest magic by the strongest mage in all the realms couldn't remove every piece of glitter from the front of your shirt. I'm sorry to break it to you, but you will forever be sparkling."

Shade threw his hands down beside him, energy rolling from his wrists down his palms. He lifted his arms in the air and long strings of magic, hundreds of them, flew up toward the hole in the ceiling. They spread out and began to work as if they were small construction workers, mending and filling the holes and gaps until there was no sign of the hole that had just been there. When that was done, he shifted his arms down at the collapsed coffee table and began mending that as well. Within seconds everything was back to the way it was before, except for the massive amount of glitter covering him. He brushed at it again and then shook his head. "I'm sorry. I didn't mean to come plummeting through your roof."

"Teleportation troubles?" Willa asked.

I shook my head sarcastically. "I'm telling you, if you just let go of your pride and rode a broom like every other witch, you'd have much gentler landings."

Willa giggled and Shade just stared at me, blinking wildly. "Really? You're still on the broom thing?"

I pointed at the hot glue gun still stuck to his pants. "It's better than being stuck on the glue thing... Or the glitter train... Or the construction paper stuck to your back."

Shade struggled for a few more moments, ripping things off him and tossing them on the table. Willa and I both had to stop ourselves from laughing. Mr. Hobbles jumped up next to Willa and sat down, beginning to lick his fur. "I officially ban all glitter from this house. The cauldron keeper over there landed right in the middle of your pile and threw it all over me like Napalm."

Willa stuck out her bottom lip at him and patted him on the top of the head. She turned her gaze back to Shade who had remarkably removed most of the glitter at that point. "So, why exactly did you come falling through the roof of Callie's house? You know there's a front door, right?"

Shade rolled his shoulders and twisted his neck back and forth. "Like I said, I didn't mean to land that way. I teleported in a hurry, and somehow I miscalculated and came through halfway in your roof."

I walked over and sat on the edge of the couch looking down at the glitter and the carpet. "I suppose it's better than coming through the portal midway through one of us. Though it might have been a little bit easier to clean up than this glitter."

Shade winced at the thought. "That would've

been mortifying. Though, not so much if it had been your cat."

Mr. Hobbles growled deeply at him and jumped down, scurrying off into the kitchen. Shade looked back at the two of us. "Look, as much as I want to sit and chat and catch up, I'm here for a reason. I received word just a moment ago that my brother and your father were seen in the witch world."

Willa's face went serious and she jumped up from the couch. "What? When? That means they're in this realm and it may be our only chance to get them back."

Shade nodded. "That's what I was thinking, and on our terms. Apparently, they were spotted not long ago but the merchant that told me was really scared, and I couldn't get much more out of him. Our city isn't that big, so it should be pretty easy to find them."

"Hold on," I said, putting up my hand. "You said they're in the witch world, but then Willa said they're in this realm. There's a specific area of this realm that's just for witches?"

Willa hurried over to me and grabbed my wrist, pulling me up from the couch. "We can ex- plain all that later. Let's go pack bags so that we have our stuff with us and then Shade can take us back."

I glanced up at Shade, my cheeks feeling warm as his gaze moved over me. "As long as we can try not to land in the middle of a roof or someone's artistic creations."

"I'm never going to hear the end of this, am I?" Shade replied with a frown.

I shook my head. "Not for a while. You did it to yourself. If you hadn't been so brooding the entire time we've known you, and cracked a joke or made a mistake somewhere along the way, I might let this one go. But this is too good."

Willa rolled her eyes and started to pull me down the hallway. "Just pack for a little while, just normal clothes and whatever toiletries you want. Luckily the witches are in this realm, so it'll be easy for us to move back and forth. I'll call one of the Fae to come check on the animals while we're gone." She began to walk toward the bathroom and stopped, turning back to me. "You don't have to go with us if you don't want to…"

I sarcastically wiped my hand across my forehead. "Well, that's a relief. Don't be stupid. Of course I'm coming with you. Grab my shampoo, toothbrush, and deodorant, and I'll load up two bags for us."

Willa smiled, hurrying into the bathroom, and

I went into my room, leaving the door open. I pulled out my drawers and began to pull things out, realizing that I wasn't even stopping to think what I should wear around Shade. Sure, I was still full of butterflies, and even standing there covered in glue and glitter he was hot, but my mind was on the task at hand and I wasn't even sure what we were going to be facing when we got there. All I knew was that it was a chance to get Willa's dad and Shade's brother back, and if I could help in any way, I would. If I hadn't had that bracelet, I was sure they wouldn't let me go, but there was still something very suspicious about the bracelet clinging to me, and I knew it was connected with what was going on. I couldn't say that my powers were stronger than everyone else's, but the bracelet was working through me and I had seen the look on both Willa and Shade's faces when it had come to life in front of them.

By the time Willa got back with all the toiletries, I had packed my bag and hers. Luckily, I knew her all too well and had packed all of her favorite clothes, but left out the things I knew would be less than comfortable if we were running from a horde of evil magic demons. I sat down on the edge of the bed and slipped my feet into my boots, lacing them up. Willa changed out of her llama pajamas and I threw a sweatshirt on over the T-shirt I was wearing. Grabbing a brush, I pulled my hair back into a ponytail and shrugged as I glanced at myself in the mirror. Yes, they were the clothes I had gone to bed in, but I hadn't been asleep very long, and they weren't that much different than the clothes I wore when I wasn't in bed.

Willa walked up next to me and brushed her hair, pushing her glasses up her nose. "You ready for another adventure?"

"I feel like a Hobbit," I replied. "But yeah, I'm ready. I feel like we've been living in limbo these past few weeks and I know that we'll continue living that way until we find your father and Shade's brother. As much as I'd like to go back to a quiet life, I'm not sure that I'll ever be able to again. At least not in the way that I had been before."

Willa turned toward me and stepped forward, wrapping her arms around me. She hugged me tightly and rested her chin on my shoulder. "That's not necessarily a bad thing. But in order to get to that point, we all have to survive. So, when we're there, try not to go off on your own or get kidnapped again. I know you don't have much control over that, but the magic in that bracelet seems to be growing stronger and I don't know anything about it, but I would think that you'd be able to eventually work with it and use it to your advantage. Maybe that's something the witches can help with. They have experience with totems and other magical devices."

"What's a totem?"

"It's like an object that has magic transferred into it. Witches are able to take the magic from those items or use the items in a magical way. The magic doesn't have to be theirs. It's illegal to do it now because there were some bad witches a long time ago who were stealing magic from witches and Fae and sticking them in totems."

I looked down at the bracelet. "Is this a totem?"

She put her hand over the bracelet and smiled at me. "It's a little bit more complicated than that, but for all intents and purposes, yeah." Both Willa and I looked over our shoulders toward the bedroom door as we heard Shade and Mr. Hobbles arguing over something. Willa rolled her eyes and I chuckled. She squeezed my wrist and then let go. "We can talk about all that later. Let's break up this fight and get out of here. I think, if my timing's right, we should be able to get a few hours of searching in before it gets dark where they are."

I slung the bag over my shoulder and followed Willa to the door. "I always did want to travel internationally, just not as some detective sleuth facing bad guys. But hey, it's definitely a story I'll be able to tell my grandchildren if I ever have any."

Out in the living room, Mr. Hobbles had jumped onto the back of the couch and was staring up at Shade who had his hands on his hips, shaking his head dramatically. "I don't understand why you'd want to go."

"Why I want to go is none of your business," Mr. Hobbles replied. "All you need to know is that you don't have a choice in this. I'm not going to be left behind again."

"Where are you going?" I asked Mr. Hobbles.

He walked along the back of the couch and rubbed his face against my arm. "I'm going with you to the witch world."

I looked up at Shade who rolled his eyes and shrugged. "I guess, why not? He will blend right in with the rest of the cats. I will tell you this though, Mr. Hobbles, if you get in the way or you find yourself in a dangerous situation, I'm going to pick Willa and Callie over you, even if that means you're turned into a pile of dust and fur."

Mr. Hobbles began to purr. "That's fair enough. So, when do we leave?"

Willa put up her finger as she pulled the phone to her ear. "Hey, can you do me a favor?"

I looked over at Shade. "She's calling one of the Fae to come take care of the animals… Or just the dog, I guess. Oh, and probably open up the shop tomorrow."

Shade looked at his watch and then around the room, impatience boiling over from his persona. Willa turned away from him, but didn't say anything. She knew he was impatient and she knew why, but that didn't mean we didn't have to take care of things where we were. Unfortunately, we couldn't just transport back and forth and not have somebody look after the shop and Bean. "Thank you, we really appreciate it. The spare key is under the planter in front of Callie's house, and you have a key to the shop. I'm not sure how long we'll be, but hopefully, fingers crossed, by the time we come back we'll have a really good idea of where the King is, or even have him with us maybe. We'll come back here before we go to the Fae realm if we get him. I know you want to go back for a little bit."

I was assuming it was probably Bailey who she was talking to. The other Fae missed the Fae realm even more than we did. Who could be mad at that? That was their home and they left to protect the Princess, something they cared about, but they still left all their family and friends behind. I couldn't imagine it was an easy thing to go through.

Willa hung up the phone and turned it off, shoving it in her back pocket. She looked over at me and gave a nod. I reached down, picking Mr. Hobbles up and holding him close to my chest. His heart was beating rapidly and I could tell that he was nervous, but I wasn't really sure why. Maybe it was the teleportation. It definitely made me nervous, but mostly because I didn't want to puke in front of Shade. You would think it would be like old hat to me now, but it seemed the less I did it, the more it affected me, and I hadn't been transporting anywhere over the last few weeks.

Shade, Willa, Mr. Hobbles, and I gathered together in the middle of the room. Shade nodded toward Mr. Hobbles. "You'll want to put him down. You don't want a weird situation where we come out on the other side and he's physically part of you."

My eyes went wide and I quickly set him down. "No, I really would not want my talking cat to be part of my physical body."

"For the love of the Queen, please no," Mr. Hobbles replied. "It would be my luck that I was stuck on her backside the whole time. Or right by her mouth. I would have to hear every human word that came out of her."

I looked down and narrowed my eyes at him. "If I pick him up and toss him while we're in worm hole thingy, will we be able to emerge on the other side and turn him into a feline glitter bomb?"

Mr. Hobbles gasped and both Shade and Willa chuckled. I winked at Mr. Hobbles and smiled, turning my attention back to the three of them. Shade put his hand out and Willa and I pressed ours over his, with Mr. Hobbles setting his paw on my foot. As Shade began to whisper his magic spell, I closed my eyes, hoping that would help with the transition into the portal. Hope was about all I had because once we moved from our living room into the portal between realms and space, I could feel my stomach flip-flop. I kept my eyes shut though, at least until I felt something else. Suddenly, a chilling five fingers gripped tightly to my warm skin, flowing the cold through my meat and muscle, and down to the bone. It moved quickly up to my shoulder and down my spine.

Opening my eyes, I found a frail and bony, skeleton-like hand wrapped around my wrist. The skin was almost translucent and its nails were long and curled. With the whole entire essence of space and time whizzing past me, coupled with an unlikely intruder, I didn't know what to do at first. I called out but my voice seemed to not travel past my lips. It was as if there was a void blocking all sound from the portal. I didn't know if that was normal or not because the last few times I had transported with Shade, it had been so quick that I had barely any time to think about it. Not to mention that all of my focus was on not puking.

But this time, the icy hand on my wrist had woken me to my surroundings and I could feel the hand pulling me toward the edge of the portal. I was suspended within the racing tunnel of space and time, and I had nothing but my own strength to pull back with. But the hand was strong and I couldn't see much more than a little bit of its wrist and forearm. I couldn't tell what kind of creature had a hold of me and I couldn't see or hear what it wanted. But I knew in the pit of my stomach, just as I had for days, that whatever it wanted, it wasn't good.

I had no idea what would happen if I was suddenly pulled through the portal into another realm. Would I be ripped apart? Would I be lost forever with no one knowing where I had gone? Whatever the creature was, would it even let me survive long enough to find out? Fear began to palpitate my heart, and though I could feel the bracelet strongly vibrating against my skin, the magic of whatever the creature was seemed to push it back down, not allowing it to take hold. Everything in me was growing colder and colder, and my breaths began to cloud as they came from my chest. Whatever the creature was, it was freezing me to death. I could feel its icy grasp moving further and further through my body, and I didn't know how to stop it.

I knew that I was going to be in danger no matter where we went, but never even making it to the witch world hadn't been on my radar at all. I knew nothing about portals, or the creature that had a grasp me. But what I did know was, I was in trouble and if I didn't get away, I may never see Willa or Shade again. I wouldn't be much help to them if I was lost in another realm or worse, dead. I really wasn't ready to be dead.

The energy coming from the cold hand increased and my eyes started to grow blurry. My strength was waning, and I had a feeling that I wasn't going to be able to fight whatever the creature was off of me. At least I wasn't going to be able to do it in the portal. The only thing was, I was pretty sure that wherever I came out, if I did, I'd be dead before I had a chance to even try.

4

Shade

A USUAL TRIP transporting through the portal takes seconds, but as I looked around me, and felt the absence of any sound, I knew something wasn't right.

A cold chill flowed through the air and I turned, looking back at where Callie was. Instead of freely flowing through the portal like she was supposed to, she was frozen, and not just physically frozen but temperature-wise as well. Gripping to her wrist was a pale bony hand and her skin was turning a light shade of blue with frost covering her from her fingertips to her shoulders. Her mouth was open and I could see her attempting to struggle, but whatever had grasped her had a hold of her and it wasn't letting go.

Using my magic, I slowed myself, reaching for Callie before the creature could pull her through the portal and into another realm. Being a human, I wasn't sure that she would survive that, and I would never be able to find her. Growing closer, I was finally able to grab onto her hand, and touching it, I found her to be as cold as ice. Her breathing was slowing, and the creature was killing her, whether it meant to or not.

Fighting against the pressure of the portal, feeling a sense of the witch castle coming close, I mustered my energy and slammed my hand down against the creature's. A bright white light flashed and rippled outward, jolting my hand from hers. I reached back, and just as the creature let go, I grabbed her wrist and flung her toward our exit. I turned my head as I exited as well, wanting to see if I could catch a glimpse of the creature, but I couldn't. It had disappeared back into its realm, or wherever it had come from.

Feeling the boundary between our world and the portal, I crossed my arms over my chest and closed my eyes. I hit the ground with a thud, knocking the wind from my lungs. Quickly, I opened my eyes and found that I had landed us right in the yard in front of the house. I hadn't even really been focused on where to go, so I was surprised we weren't a hundred miles away, on the other side of Rome in the country.

Thoughts of Callie immediately struck me and I jumped up, looking around for her. I found her on her hands and knees about fifty feet away, groaning as she pulled herself to her feet. Her skin was back to its pale color and any remnants of ice were gone, except for one dried tear, crystallized on her cheek, but it quickly melted and she wiped it away.

I raced toward her and grabbed her by the elbow just as she stumbled to the side trying to get her balance. I turned her toward me and looked her up and down just to make sure she was okay. She seemed a little bit out of it but when her eyes met mine, she shook her head. "What... What was that?"

From behind us we heard Willa calling out. Callie and I looked back at her as she was running toward us. Callie gripped my forearms and I looked down into her eyes again. "Don't tell Willa. Not until we know what happened. It will only worry her. She's got enough going on."

Before I could argue with her, Willa was upon us, and I figured that Callie knew what was best for Willa more than I did. Willa chuckled and squeezed Callie's shoulder. "You'll never get used to the portals, will you?"

Callie forced a laugh, her eyes darting to mine and back to Willa's. "I guess I won't. I'll be okay though. Just as long as we don't do that again anytime soon."

Willa shook her head. "We shouldn't. You should have a rest period first."

I cleared my throat and looked around at the morning sun. It was late morning, almost the afternoon. "Maybe you guys could lay down and rest for a little bit. Even for the Fae, traveling through teleportation can be exhausting. We can go first thing in the morning to inspect and question people."

Willa shook her head, tightening the straps on her bag. "No, it's early in the day, much earlier than I thought it would be. I want to go right out and do some investigation. The more time that we lose, the further away my father and your brother could get. We don't know how much time they have. If they're here in this realm still, we might be able to find them. I don't think it would be wise for us to take too much of a rest."

She looked to Callie who was rubbing her arms and noticed the goosebumps on them. "You can rest though. Lay down in the castle and have something to eat. We'll be back soon."

Callie shook her head. "Of course not. I'll be fine. I want to find them as much as you do. Well, I want to find them a lot. Look, for whatever reason, I was pulled into this and maybe I'll find out why one day or maybe I won't, but Willa, I told you you're my family and I'll help you with anything that you need. I don't need to be taken care of like I'm fragile. I know I'm a human, but right now, I have magic too. And I can feel my bracelet pulsing energy into me as we speak. It's like having an IV of energy drink at all times. I could've used this in college."

Willa laughed and put her arm over Callie's shoulder. "I knew you were stubborn, but I love you for it."

"I can take you to your room so you can at least drop off your things before we go," I suggested, trying to give Callie just a little bit more time to get herself together. I wasn't sure whether she was lying about the bracelet or not, but her cheeks were looking rosy again and her eyes were wider.

We started to walk toward the castle and

Callie slowed. "I do have one concern. The last time I was here, I had a really hard time with communication. I don't speak Italian or French and most of the people down in the city, in Rome, besides the tourists, don't speak English. That's what ended up putting me in the alleyway with the King Collector last time. Of course, I was also running from that guy at the same time."

Willa clicked her tongue and shook her head at me. "Look what you did."

I rolled my eyes. "That won't be a problem where we're going."

Callie furled her brow. "Oh, was I just in the wrong part of Rome?"

I glanced over at Willa and she glanced back at me, a smirk on both of our faces. Willa walked up to Callie and took her hand. "We're not going to Rome, Callie. The witches have their very own world here."

Callie looked confused. "So, like a hidden magical world? Right here in my realm? Please don't tell me that we're going to platform 9 ¾. I am not running at a brick wall. I am not that lucky."

Willa and I both leaned our heads back and laughed excitedly. I shook my head at Willa. "You really didn't teach her anything about our worlds since you've been back, have you?"

Willa shrugged. "Yeah, well, I've been a little bit busy protecting her, dealing with running a business, thinking about my missing father, having conversations with a cat and dog..."

Callie gasped and we both turned back toward her. "Mr. Hobbles! Where's Mr. Hobbles? He came through the portal with us but I don't see him anywhere."

Willa, Callie and I glanced at the front of the house, wondering if maybe he had reappeared inside. I had sent all of us to the same spot but things were a little shifty inside the portal so it wasn't a surprise to me that Willa had landed in a different area. However, as we went to walk forward, calling for Mr. Hobbles, someone with a deep voice groaned behind us. I looked over at Callie who had stopped in her tracks, her eyes shifting over toward me. "What was that?"

The groan sounded out again behind us and we all slowly turned around. Lying on the ground, completely naked, with bits of fur pressed to his skin, was a man. He had dark hair with white patches, and his fingers were digging into the dirt as he attempted to pull himself up. Before he could, he let out a deep breath and collapsed back to the ground, turning his head toward us.

He blinked at Callie several times. "Haven't been in this body in a long time."

Immediately, I put my arm out and pushed Callie back behind me, letting the magic flow to my hands. Willa stepped up next to me, glancing over at me and then back to the man. "Is he one of yours?"

"I can sense magical ability, but also... Also..."

Willa tapped me on the shoulder. "Also what?"

I chuckled nervously as I ran my hand through my hair. I didn't know how to say it. I sensed magic, but I also sensed hints of a feline variety. He wasn't a Shifter but he was confusing my senses. I couldn't tell if he was doing it on purpose or if it was just naturally coming off that way. I cleared my throat and stepped forward. "Where did you come from?"

He looked to be in his late forties, his arms strong and lean, and I watched as he pushed himself up, struggling until he was on his feet, or actually on his foot. Naked, he brushed the dirt off himself and hobbled up and down, missing one of his legs. "That's a bit more of a confusing story, love. However, what I'm more curious about right now is if the taste of tuna fish will ever get out of my mouth. And I'm pretty sure I'm due for a hair-ball at any time. That's not going to be very pretty coming out of this body."

I could feel Callie's hand push against my shoulder as she stepped between me and Willa. She had a look of shock on her face and her eyes were narrowed, staring at him. She looked like she wanted to say something, but nothing was coming out. I was starting to think she was in shock. After several moments of staring at him though, she swallowed hard and shook her head, blinking her eyes. She looked to me and then over to Willa and back at the man. "I'm not going crazy right? You guys both see a naked guy, with one leg, hopping up and down in front of us, right?"

"Unfortunately," Willa said, sneering as he continued to bounce up and down. "Whoever he is, I would like to formally request that the witches give him some pants before we continue questioning him any further."

The man let out a relieved sigh. "Yes, please. Please tell me you have a good tailor here. I knew one before, but I believe he's still in London. If he's even still alive. Good chap, very good tailor. I'm really glad that suit tails are no longer a thing. I always got them caught on things."

Callie's mouth dropped wide open and she took two steps forward, with both Willa and I reaching out for her. She shook her head at us and stared at the man, shock but no fear on her face. The man put his hands in front of him and stood up straight, trying not to wobble on his one leg.

As Callie took another step forward, she cupped her hands over her mouth and shook her head. "Mr. Hobbles, is that you?"

Holy hell, I did not see that coming.

5

Callie

I HAVE TO ADMIT, if you told me that Mr. Hobbles was really a human, the man bouncing up and down in front of me was not what I would've imagined.

Then again, if you told me that Mr. Hobbles was a human before I knew about Willa, I would've given you a warm blanket and taken you to the hospital. It never seemed to fail that when one thing weird happened about 700 other things followed. As if the cold hand in the portal wasn't enough, now I was staring at a forty-something, tall, strong, and lean naked man, bouncing up and down on one leg, talking about his favorite tailor in London.

He lifted both hands up and out to the side, giving me a smile. "It's me." He wavered back and forth and stuck up one finger. "Hold on just one second for me."

I lifted both brows, finding it odd that he wasn't at least alarmed in the slightest by the fact that we were finding out he was human, had tricked us into coming to the witch's castle, and I had two very powerful magical beings staring him down ready to take him out. Willa and Shade looked at each other, confused. Mr. Hobbles, or whatever his name was, rubbed his hands together and closed his eyes, whispering to himself. He pulled his hands apart and began to move them in the most elegant manner I'd ever seen. He waved them through the air, streams of magic falling from his palms more fluidly than I had ever seen from Shade or Willa. The magic blanketed him, first filling in the space between his knee and the ground, creating a magical fake leg.

Once that was in place and he had, for all intents and purposes, two solid feet on the ground, the magic then spun him very regal clothing. He wore a pair of black trousers, shiny black shoes, a matching vest, a button up white shirt, and to round it out, an ascot. The magic even removed the white from his hair and scruffy beard. He suddenly looked like a new man, a rich snobby English one, which let me know that he was telling the truth.

He ran his hands up through his short black hair, slowly opening and closing his emerald - green eyes. "Now there. That's much better. Do you know how annoying it is to lick your own ass every day?"

Shade snickered and I shot him an angry glance. Turning back to the man, I crossed my arms over my chest and stomped forward. "Who are you? Where's my cat?"

He immediately straightened up, pulled on his ascot a bit, and cleared his throat. "Oh, yes. You'd probably like me to explain."

"That would be preferable," I replied with irritation.

"Sir Walter Concorde, but you may call me Sir Hobbles if it helps you remember my name."

He extended his arm and his hand to shake, but I kept my hands firmly gripping my arms and stared down at it, as if he thought I would actually shake his hand. I was furious. No, more than that, I wanted to break him. He had been there for some of the most intimate moments of my life, from tears to laughter and everything in between, and the entire time, he was really a man. Shade walked up next to me and put his hand on my shoulder, giving me a look as if he could tell what was going through my mind. He turned back to Sir Hobbles, shaking his hand and his head at the same time. "I'm sorry, but did you say Sir Walter Concorde?"

As if he were proud to be recognized, Sir Hobbles gripped onto the inside of the top of his vest and lifted his chin. "None other."

Shade looked back at Willa who shrugged her shoulders. When he turned back to Sir Hobbles, he took a moment to process before speaking. "Sir Walter Concorde... As in the Wizard that ended the Great War of the Dark over 700 years ago? The Sir Walter Concorde that everyone said died?"

Hobbles let out a long deep sigh, his shoulders slumping a bit. "Is that what they've been saying? That's a pity. But yes, that was me. The great battle had raged for over eight years, and I had been on the front lines the entire time. I had fought next to some of the greatest wizards and magical beings in history. Everyone said that I was invincible, they were convinced of it, but I wasn't. I followed alongside great men, and I caught a few lucky breaks. When it came down to the last great battle, it was me and the Dark Warlock."

I looked between Shade and Hobbles and couldn't tell whether Shade was looking at him like he was crazy or if he was starstruck. Nonetheless, whatever story he was telling sounded like a fairy tale or movie.

Hobbles looked up at the sky, his eyes darkening a bit. "That last battle went on for eight hours. There were no breaks, no weapons, just magic against magic. I wielded light magic, which everyone knows is a combination of light and dark to balance, but the Dark Warlock only dabbled in the darkest of magic. It had begun to rain and I had swiftly hidden myself behind a large stone, trying to catch my breath. I had been hit across the arm. I had been splattered with dark magic pins and needles, and I was feeling myself draining of magic quickly. I knew the battle was almost over, but even I wasn't sure who would win in that moment. As I stood there, pressing my back against the cold stone, I watched as the rain began to wash the blood from all of my fallen brothers and sisters into the soil to continue the cycle of life."

He breathed deeply and turned his gaze back to Shade.

"I thought about every face I'd seen along the way, every person I had gotten close to, and not a single one of them had survived. But as you all may know, light magic has a little trick up its natural sleeves. I called on all the fallen and asked them to stand with me so that if I fell, I didn't have to be alone. When I stepped out from behind that stone, the Dark Warlock didn't just look at me battered and bruised, he watched as tens, no, hundreds of thousands of magical soldiers stood beside me and behind me for as far as the eye could see. They were spirits and they had come to show their support. It gave me that one last push I needed to make it through."

He pulled the ascot down, revealing a scar on his throat.

"The time difference between when I let off my magical shot versus his couldn't have been more than a few milliseconds, too short of a time to even count. I saw as my shot struck him and he wailed so loudly that it shook the ground. And as his shot spiraled toward me, I made peace with the idea that I would never again see a world without war, but never again would the Dark

Warlock taunt the lands and kill our people. I closed my eyes, readying myself for what came next, and I felt the shot hit me, but it wasn't a lethal blow. The spirits of the soldiers had surrounded me and used their own magic to decrease the spell that was flying toward me. But it did hit me. It hit me and did something that no one saw coming. I was thankful it wasn't a lethal blow, but unfortunately, it also turned me into a cat."

"Is that how you lost your leg?" Willa asked from behind us.

Shade shook his head. "He lost his leg in battle, and from what the history books say, he took the very thread from the enemy's clothing and sewed himself up on the battlefield. Then he enchanted a magical leg to continue fighting."

Hobbles nodded his head. I pursed my lips, still pissed off but curious. "So, that battle was where?"

He put his arms out and turned in a circle. "Why it was right here. Of course, there wasn't a giant mansion, and we stayed a little bit further back so that the nomads of the area wouldn't see us. But this is the first time I've stood on this field since I was turned into a cat."

"So, you were turned into a cat here, but how

did you get all the way out to California where I adopted you?"

Hobbles pointed at me and smiled. "Good question. I wandered the dusty and dirty streets, watching them turn from dirt roads into stone roads, and eventually into what they are today. I ate rats and trash for hundreds of years. When they were building this mansion, one of the witches created a portal to go visit their family. When they opened the portal, they didn't do it how you just did it, Shade. They used to actually open portals, but some witches weren't as talented as the others and they put a stop to that because they were opening portals to the wrong places and allowing enemies to enter by accident. Many witches died just from large furry beasts from other realms gobbling them up as soon as they opened the portal. Anyway, I jumped through the portal and it led me to where you live."

"And then you spent all of that time until I adopted you, roaming the streets?"

Hobbles took a deep breath and shrugged. "It's been an interesting 700 or so years. I found a home every now and then, would be a good cat to my owner until they passed away of old age, astounded by how old I was which was usually older than them. I had a couple of owners that I missed dearly, but I liked my freedom at the same time. And then, eight years ago, the pound caught me and that's where you adopted me from."

I glanced over at Willa who was staring at me, both of us having a hard time believing what was happening. I pinched the bridge of my nose. "So, if you were a human, why didn't you turn yourself back earlier than now?"

"You're brighter than I gave you credit for as a cat. I had to get back to the witch castle. Or, within the realm of the witch magic. I had studied on my own for years and years about how to reverse the spell, so I was just biding my time until I could make it back here. It was really very simple. It was an herbal cocktail which was kind of difficult to put together with two paws, but I managed and I drank it right before we left. Then as soon as we were within witch magic, it reversed it. So here I am."

I mumbled softly, "Here you are." I stood there staring at him for some time before the realizations began to hit. I imagined my everyday life and how many times I had walked past Hobbles and not even thought about it. Suddenly, my eyes went wide and I wrapped my arms around myself gasping. "You... I changed in front of you! I showered! I went to the restroom in front of you!! I..."

I decided to stop there, as Shade was already staring at me wondering what I was going to say next. Hobbles put his hand across his stomach and bowed. "I promise you that everything that happened while I lived with you will remain under strict confidence until I die."

I blinked rapidly, mouthing the words he had just said. Suddenly though, I snapped. I lunged toward him, wanting to rip the ascot right off his neck. I'd been angry at Mr. Hobbles before, but never that angry. Unfortunately, Shade was fast and he grabbed me around the waist, pulling me back. I looked at Shade angrily. "He knows my most intimate moments. He was a human the whole time, and for part of that he could even talk, and he never told me."

"Wait," Hobbles said, looking between us. "I believe there's a bit of a misunderstanding. You see Callie, when humans are turned to animals, or witches in my case, we inhabit the animal's mind as well. We're able to keep a certain degree of our human conscious but not to the level of understanding. My time at your house is a blur. I don't remember a lot of it. Actually, I barely remember any of it. It's a sort of kind gesture thrown in by those that use the spell. Otherwise, if we had full consciousness, it would be complete torture. We wouldn't function. Even our bodies would fail because our mind wouldn't understand. So, while I say that your secrets are safe with me, it is because I care about your privacy, but mostly because I don't remember anything."

"What about when you started talking?"

Hobbles nodded his head and Shade slowly let go of me, making sure I wasn't going to pounce on him again. Hobbles took a deep breath. "When you gave me my voice, my conscious mind came back."

Willa walked up next to me, her arms now crossed over her chest. "It's been weeks, a couple months even since I gave you your voice back. While I can't currently remember a moment where you were in a situation with us that we should feel embarrassed about, I can't understand why you wouldn't tell us then. If you knew you could become human again by just getting to the witch world, then why didn't you tell someone so we could get you there?"

Hobbles pursed his lips, his eyes shifting from Shade to me and over to Willa. He looked nervous, like he was hiding something. Willa took a step toward him, narrowing her eyes. Her arms came down by her sides and her hands curled into fists. "Why did you want to go to the Fae world so badly? If you're a witch, why wouldn't you be trying to get here instead? I distinctly remember you arguing and arguing to go to the Fae world."

Hobbles swallowed hard, backing up as Willa walked forward. He put his hands up in defense. "Calm down now."

Willa looked him up and down, and stepped back next to me, putting her hand on my wrist. "I don't buy this phony act at all. I don't buy that you're some poor lost wizard. Maybe you are, but that doesn't explain why you would want to come to the Fae world. During the Great Wars, we were not allies."

Hobbles' face grew still, almost eerie, and angry. His cheek twitched and his brow furrowed as he curled his lips into a mischievous grin.

He took a step toward us, and Shade turned to face him, putting his arms out in front of me and Willa. Mr. Hobbles kept his eyes glued on Willa. "Because the enemy has always eluded me…"

6

Callie

"So, what? Are you like some British, what, 007?" I asked, pushing Shade's arm away and stepping forward.

I wasn't afraid of Hobbles even though I probably should've been. "You were using your long-time curse to infiltrate the Fae?"

Hobbles' eyebrow went up and his arms dropped just before he burst into laughter. It lightened the situation a little bit, and Willa stepped back, confused at his reaction. Hobbles shook his head as he gathered himself. "No, not at all. I could tell as a cat that there was something familiar about Willa, but I didn't realize what it was until she gave me a voice and my consciousness back. It was only then that I saw how much the Fae had changed. Willa was kind, loving, and rejected the old ways of the Fae."

He put his hands together and tapped his fingers against his lips. "You probably haven't read the history of the witches, but I was one of the very first advocates a thousand years ago for the alliance between the Fae and the witches. It wasn't until after the Great War that they found a common ground, but I was gone. I was curious. I wanted to see what the Fae had turned into. I wanted to see if they were as kind as Willa was and if everything I had fought for was worth it. I meant no harm to Willa or you. To be honest, I saw my opening to be free of that cat body, and up until meeting Willa, I was bitter toward the Fae. The last one I saw was on the battlefield and he cut my leg off with Fae magic."

Willa's face softened and her arms hung loosely at her sides. I could tell that she felt almost bad about suspecting him of something negative, but I didn't blame her for it. The whole situation seemed very strange. At the same time, from the look in his eyes, I could tell that he was being sincere. After all, human body or cat body, it didn't really matter, I knew the real Hobbles.

He carefully took a step forward and clasped his hands in front of him. "I believe I can be helpful. I'd like to join your team, or continue being part of it. I've been watching and waiting for 700 years, but the most memorable part of it were the last eight that I've been with you. Callie, I'm your protector. I guess in a way, I've become your familiar. You aren't a witch, but you're as close to one as I have seen in a long time. Even in my cat mind I longed for my people. But the truth of it is, my fate is bound to that bracelet. When the bracelet comes off of you, I go back to being a cat. It's just how the spell works. You're ultimately my keeper. But I feel that I've been brought to you for a purpose."

I bit the inside of my cheek, trying not to feel the emotions that wanted to cloud me. I hadn't realized how I was sitting there getting angry at him, when he had spent the last eight years protecting me. Willa took a deep breath and lowered her head. "You may not be my favorite furball, but anyone who protects Callie, they receive my protection and thanks. I appreciate it."

Hobbles gave Willa a warm smile and nodded his head. I could tell he wanted to reach out to

Willa, but he didn't dare. He was still worried that she may just snap and use her Fae magic on him. I couldn't imagine that the Fae that cut off his leg looked anything like Willa or acted like her, but it wasn't about the body type, it was about the magic within them, and Willa, in the Fae realm, was incredibly powerful.

I looked over at Shade, but he was just standing there shaking his head, still awestruck. "All of this time, after all the searches, the witches thought you were long dead. We would've never stopped looking if we had known."

It was obvious from Shade's stature, and the fact that he bowed to Hobbles, that the man standing in front of him was revered. I couldn't think of a single person in human history that would get that kind of response if they suddenly showed up again after having been dead for 700 years.

Hobbles walked forward and put his hand on Shade's shoulder. "I didn't know until he had changed me that I was basically immortal as a cat. Who knows how long I would've lived? I had far more than nine lives, that's for sure."

Everyone stood there in the quiet for a moment and Willa and I glanced back and forth at each other, not wanting to ruin the moment between Shade and Hobbles. But the day was moving on, and there were important things to be done. I knew that I could get more out of Hobbles later, but if he wanted to help find the kings, I would welcome the help.

"So, while this is a really interesting moment and everything, and my mind is a little bit blown from knowing all this, we still have a really important thing to do." I gave Shade a kind smile.

He nodded, straightened himself out, his brooding look moving back over his face. "You're right. Let's get your things inside, and then we will head over to the city. It would be our honor if you would stay here, Sir Concorde."

Hobbles patted Shade on the back and nodded. "Thank you."

Being back at the witch castle was a little bit strange. It was awfully familiar to me, and I liked it also because it brought me close to Shade. Despite everything that had happened in the last few hours, there was still a part of me that was really excited to see him. I kept it to myself though, knowing that last time it drove me crazy how he pulled me in and then pushed me away. I wanted to protect myself from that here. I wanted to be totally on the case and helping to find Shade and Willa's kings.

Shade put me in the same room that I had been in the last time I was there, and Callie across the hall. He took Hobbles to a different wing, probably much fancier than the one we were staying in, though it was the fanciest place I had ever been. Well, up until I went to the Fae castle that was. I changed out of my sweatshirt into a tank top and freshened up a little bit before meeting Callie back in the hallway. As we walked toward the front door to meet everyone else, I took a deep breath, fiddling with my fingers.

Willa glanced over at me. "You okay?"

I gave her a smile. "Yeah, just a lot to take in. It's always a lot to take in."

Willa chuckled. "I have to say, this time I'm as shocked as you. I'm sorry that you have to keep getting this mind-blowing information from everywhere, but at least you're checking off the boxes and eventually there won't be much to shock you with anymore."

We both laughed, but on the inside, I knew I wasn't talking about Hobbles. I was still thinking about the ice-cold hand that had grabbed me in the portal earlier. I felt almost as if it had left a lingering effect on me. It was weird, like I could still sense the being, whatever it was.

As we walked out of the castle, I stopped at

the top of the stairs. "Where are the SUVs? I thought we were going to the secret witchy town."

"We are," Shade said from behind us.

I turned around and smiled, finding that he had changed his clothes too. I quickly dropped the smile though, not wanting to seem ridiculous. Unfortunately, Willa had seen it and she giggled, elbowing me in the side. "How are we getting there?"

Shade took a deep breath, and I could tell he knew I wasn't going to like his answer. "I was going to have us drive there, but we spent so much time with the whole Hobbles situation that we should probably teleport so that we don't lose any more daylight."

I wrinkled my nose and nodded my head, not at all wanting to do it. I didn't know what to expect. If one creature could come after me, how many others would start coming after me when they realized that the bracelet I was wearing was far more powerful than even I could understand. Hobbles walked out the front door, still looking as he did earlier, and rubbed his hands together. "Shall we go?"

Shade brought magic into his palms and looked at Willa and me. "Yes, but first I need you to stand still so I can put some magical cloaks over you. They will have a protection spell but they're also so the witches can't sense the Fae in you. Even you, Callie. I've sensed more Fae magic around you since you've been back than I ever had before. It must be the bracelet."

Willa and I nodded, and I stood and closed my eyes, not really thrilled to have magic swirling around me but I knew that Shade wouldn't hurt me. When he let the magic go, it whipped around us, and all I could feel was a tingling sensation against my skin. When it finally settled over my shoulders, I was wearing a long black cape with a hood up over my head. I looked at Shade curiously. "So, do the witches not dress like it's modern day?"

He shrugged. "They do, but many of them wear their ceremonial robes as well. These look like ceremonial robes. No one will think twice about it."

I nodded, following everyone down the steps and out onto the front lawn. I stood next to Shade as he put his hand out. Willa put her hand on his, Hobbles put his on top of hers, and they all looked to me. I chewed my cheek for a moment and slapped my hand on top, knowing there was no way out of it. Of course, I could tell the truth of what happened, but that wasn't going to help us find Willa's father.

Luckily, as soon as we entered into the portal, Shade turned and wrapped his arms tightly around me, pulling me close to him. I relaxed into him almost immediately, and I could feel his fingers pressing into my back. He was protecting me, but it also felt really right. The trip through the portal was a lot shorter than the last time, and when we landed, I quickly stepped away from him so that Willa and Hobbles wouldn't notice. I readied myself to take in the scene, but when I turned around, my face fell, finding nothing but a half dead open field.

My brow furled and I put my hands on my hips, turning to Shade. "Okay, not to be mean, but I have to admit this is kind of a letdown. I totally expected to fly in on a broomstick and see talking dragons and cauldrons."

Both Hobbles and Shade turned and looked at me funny. Hobbles shrugged his shoulders and went to speak, but Shade interrupted him. He threw a glance at him and then looked at me. "You seriously need to let the whole broomsticks thing go, okay?"

I put up my hands and chuckled. "What? You can deny it all you want to..."

He didn't say anything else, he just turned and stepped in front of everyone. His hands came up and he began to chant, it was some sort of magic, but in a language I didn't recognize. As he chanted, he moved forward, stopping right where the grass began to die. He spoke a couple more lines of magic and then took a large step forward. As his front leg came down, he disappeared.

"Uh, where did he go? Is this like the whole brick wall thing? Do I make a running jump?"

Hobbles laughed and stepped in front of us, walking forward and straight until he disappeared as well. I looked at Willa. "Have you done this before?"

Willa shook her head. "No. We've been around the witches, but I've never been to the city. Remember, while I was a princess and we tried to keep the peace, the whole base of our alliance was that we live in two different realms and we don't coexist. It was never truly safe for me to go in here."

I looked right and left, but there was no one else there. "So, what do we do now?"

Where Shade had entered, his head popped out, but his body was still invisible. He grinned, making my heart flutter. He stuck both hands out and nodded toward us. "Come on, it's open for you to walk through. It's really not that scary, I promise."

I narrowed my eyes at him, looking at his hand. "If this is some kind of trick, I'm going to be really mad."

Shade laughed, which was only the second time that I had ever really heard him be anything other than brooding. I liked it. I liked it probably a little bit too much. It was cool though, because I got to see more about Shade, someone who hid himself very well. He didn't like talking about himself or talking about where he came from at all. I wasn't sure I would ever see more of his life, but it looked like I was going to get to after all.

I looked over at Willa and she reached out, taking Shade's hand. I took his other hand and figured why not. At the same time, with me holding my breath, we took a step forward through the invisible barrier. I clenched my eyes shut as I stepped through, trusting that she would guide me in the right direction. Suddenly, all around me I could hear the sounds of the city, minus the cars. I could hear voices all around, the sounds of bells on doors of shops, the tapping of shoes on the hard ground, and the smell of pipe smoke and food. It reminded me of being at the farmers market when I was a kid.

"Welcome to Charm City," Hobbles said.

I opened up my eyes and immediately my mouth fell open. It was far closer to what I imagined it to be than I ever thought possible. When they said a witch city, I definitely pictured something from a fantasy movie, and it was just that. There were narrow streets, droves of people walking, all kinds of people in robes, some in regular clothes, some even wore tall pointy hats like the witches in the books. The shops were all different heights, their roofs built like the moss-covered shops in the Fae realm. Every single one of them had something different in their windows and they all had wooden signs swinging back and forth from their awning. Walking down the street amongst all the people there was an enormous, what I supposed to be, troll, towering probably twenty feet tall, lumbering along as if it was normal. People weaved in and out of his legs and he grumbled as he walked, bending down to look in different shop windows.

Of course, every troll I had ever seen was either short guarding a bridge, in a book, or enormous and wearing nothing but a loincloth, also from a book. But this troll, while large with an enormous head and button nose, and just about three strands of hair on the top of his head, was dressed in just a far larger size version of what we wore in the human realm. He had on trousers, boots, a button up white shirt, and had a large watch around his wrist. Immediately I wondered where he bought clothes like that, but I didn't think that was quite the appropriate question to ask at that moment.

Rolling down the street past us was a guy pushing a cart, and the smell that emanated from it was cinnamon and sugar. Whatever he was selling, it made my stomach rumble. I looked over at Willa, who obviously had immediately focused in on the guy with the cart. She was more of a food whore than I was. Her eyes met mine and we both nodded in agreement, knowing that we didn't have to express the fact that we were definitely going to get whatever he was selling before we left.

Shade turned toward us. "I know this is really different for the two of you, more so for you Callie probably than Willa. And while most witches are just like humans, going about our days and doing whatever we want to do, there are those that still follow the dark magic. It's important that you keep your cloaks on, because even the kindest of witches can harbor hatred for a human or a Fae. And here, the laws are different.

There will be no consequence for them if they hurt either one of you."

Slowly, Willa reached out her hand and grabbed mine, squeezing it tightly. One day, I was determined to go to a magical place where someone wasn't going to try to kill me, eat me, or steal me. It seemed like Charm City was not that place.

7

Callie

"HOW FAR DOES THE CITY GO?" Willa asked looking around.

Shade chuckled. "It's much larger than it looks. We're going to need to split up if we are going to cover ground. Hobbles do you re-member the city?"

"It doesn't seem to have changed very much, and I'm pretty sure I can make my way through. I figured we could go over to the rare trinkets and antiques part of the area just in case they were looking for anything old or rare."

Shade nodded his head. "That's perfect. Willa, why don't you go with Hobbles, and Callie can come with me."

Willa eyed Hobbles up and down for a moment and then shrugged. "Why not? Maybe you can answer some questions for me."

Hobbles smiled. "It would be my pleasure. Besides, I knew I wasn't going to get off that easily. Might as well get it over with."

Willa turned to me and put her arms around me, hugging me tightly. When she pulled away, I looked at her curiously. "What was that for?"

Willa shrugged. "I don't know. It just seems that every time we separate, we don't see each other for a while. I figured this time I'd at least give you a hug beforehand. Just be safe." She looked at Shade and pointed her finger at him. "You watch out for her."

Shade bowed to her. "Yes, your Majesty."

Hobbles chuckled but Willa threw him a glare and he immediately quieted. We gave each other one last look and turned in opposite directions. Willa and Hobbles disappeared into the crowd but Shade took me up and around the corner, down a quieter walkway. As soon as we were in the clear, Shade grabbed my arm and stopped me, turning me toward him. "What happened in the portal?"

A chill ran down my spine just thinking about it. "I really don't know. I had my eyes closed, just so I didn't get nauseous, and then I felt a cold hand on my arm. When I opened my eyes, it was grasping me, and I couldn't see its body. But as it held on, this cold floated through me and I was fighting it, but whatever it was, it was pushing down the magic of my bracelet. Before I knew it, everything was freezing. I felt like I was suffocating. Everything went dark, until there was a bright flash of light and then there you were. As soon as the hand let me go, the heat started to rush back into my body and I could breathe again."

Shade rubbed his chin, glancing around him. "I've never heard of a creature that could do that, but then again, none of us know what creatures lurk in the other realms. Has anything else weird been happening?"

I shook my head and then stopped, remembering my dream. "Actually, every night since I've been back from the Fae realm, I've had the same dream over and over again."

"Interesting," Shade mumbled. "What was it about? Where were you?"

I shook my head. "I don't know where I was. The dream starts out and I'm standing in some sort of cave and staring at an archway that's like a naturally made doorway. I'm looking for something and then I race forward, and when I run through the doorway, I'm suddenly in another place. Everything is dark and foggy, and I turn back toward the door but it's gone. That's when I realize that it's not fog around me, it's… Like ghosts. They have faces and I can hear them crying out. And then, I hear something behind me, but every time I go to turn around to see what it is, I wake from my dream."

Shade shook his head, and I could see that he was mulling over all the details. "Have you talked to the banshee yet?"

I looked at him suspiciously. "How do you know about that?"

"As soon as I stepped foot in your house, or, through your roof, I could feel its presence. I could tell it had been there for quite a while, or at least coming in and out for quite a while."

"But I thought that you put a protection on the house," I replied.

"I did, but banshees are messengers, not enemies. They don't go by the same rules of magic that everyone else does. There's a special spell to ban them from your location, but it's nothing that I'm strong enough to make. Is there anything else weird?"

I thought about it for a second and then nodded. "Yeah, right before you came, Willa was about to tell me about a dream she kept having. She said that she wasn't her in the dream but she didn't know who she was, and every time she got close to telling me where she was, or anything useful about the dream, something would interrupt us. I don't even know if it's a connection at this point, but I thought it was strange."

Shade nodded his head. "It is strange, but I don't have any more information that I can give you, not about the portal incident or the dream. But I do know what happened in the portal wasn't a dream. I saw it for myself. It may just simply be that a creature from another realm sensed your magic as we were passing by and attempted to grab you, but it could also be something more nefarious. We're just going to have to be more careful. Come on, we've got a little bit of a walk to take, and where we're going, keep your head down. The witches there aren't friendly."

Nerves rattled in my stomach but I nodded my head in understanding and turned, walking closely next to him. We took a bunch of twists and turns down different streets and then headed down a long corridor into a separate part of the city. As we entered, everything seemed to darken. The shops weren't as well taken care of, some of them didn't have signs above the windows, and every single witch that I saw wore a dark robe or tattered and worn clothing. Just the atmosphere around us felt darker.

I did notice something strange though, as we walked, several of the witches that passed by nodded their head at Shade and he seemed to recognize them. None of them looked friendly or like the kind of witches that I would find at the Castle, which made me even more curious. Everyone seemed to be nefarious there, even Shade. I wanted to ask him about it, but we were looking for specific things and I knew it wasn't the time. Plus, I didn't want him to think I suspected him of anything. I was fairly sure there were people in my life that others would've thought were nefarious as well.

About halfway down the corridor, we took a right into an even narrower walkway. At the end was an old dusty store. There was no bell on the door when we walked in, and no music filled my ears like so many of the shops in the human world. This place, though, was interesting. Everything was covered in a layer of dust, and there were stacks upon stacks of files and little bottles, no labeling on anything, filled to the brim with different potions. The air was stagnant and there was a faint smell of sulfur lingering.

In the center of the store the bottles were stacked so high that they wobbled back and forth with the breeze in the shop, but they seemed to be held together by magic. No matter how far they bent, not a single one of them fell. It was interesting, and everything in me wanted to reach out and touch it, but I knew that probably wasn't a good idea. I was pretty sure when Shade gave me the warning about where we were going, it also included not touching anything inside the stores.

To our right was a long wooden counter with an older man, turned to the side, not noticing us yet, wearing thick-lensed, round glasses, and staring carefully at a small vial he was pouring a green liquid into. His hands shook just enough for one vial to clink against the other and his tongue was partway out of his mouth as he attempted not to spill a drop.

Shade cleared his throat, and when the man turned toward us, seeing Shade's face, the mixed vial dropped from his hand. As it hit the old wooden floor, the glass broke and the dark purple liquid simmered and then congealed. Everyone stared at it for a moment, and I wondered what everyone was waiting for. But suddenly, it became clear. The congealed substance began to shake and then move, pushing out in different directions as if there were something inside trying to break free. The man pushed his glasses up his nose and stomped his black boot over top of it, chuckling nervously as he looked back up at Shade.

"Shade," he said with a shaky voice, "What brings you all the way out to my shop today? Is it something special you're looking for? I can get you anything, within the confines of the law of course."

Shade stepped forward and halfway in front of me, seeming taller and broader than before. As he spoke, his voice was deep and assertive. "Gannon, you know I don't shop here. But there is something you can help me with."

It was obvious from the first name basis and the fear radiating from Gannon that they knew each other. I could only imagine that the circumstances of why they knew each other weren't fantastic. As Shade move toward the counter, Gannon stepped back, his eyes looking down and then back up at Shade over and over again. He clasped his hands together, grabbing a rag and wiping them off. "I haven't broken the order. I've gone along with it the whole time. If somebody said I did..."

Shade cut him off. "While I doubt that you've gone along with the order, it's not what I'm here for."

Very slowly, Gannon looked up at him, studying Shade. After a few moments, his eyes darted to me, and then over at the front door. He lifted his hand and flicked his wrist. The door swung loudly shut, the bolts latching from the top of the door to the bottom. The shades on the dirty windows came slamming down, releasing balls of dust into the air. He flipped his wrist again and all of the candles that I hadn't even realized were stacked all around the room ignited.

Shade stepped forward again and opened his mouth to talk, but Gannon put his finger up and shook his head. A cascade of dark blue magic came from his finger and swirled around the shop, leaving trails all along the top edge and down each seam of the wall. Once the magic had returned to Gannon, he wiped his hand nervously again and then nodded. "You can never be too careful with who may be listening."

Shade glanced over at me and then back at Gannon, nodding his head. "That's very true. And if I find out someone is listening that you know of, someone you know I wouldn't want to be listening..." Shade walked up to the counter and put his hands on the wooden surface. The muscles in his arms flexed and he towered over Gannon. "I think we both know what will happen to you."

Gannon's hands shook wildly, and though I didn't know why Shade was treating him that way, I knew he probably had a very good reason, and I almost felt bad for the old man. Then again, he ran a shop in the seediest part of the city, selling vials of who knows what to who knows who. I couldn't imagine he had always been straightlaced. In fact, Shade was probably right, there was no way he was on the straight and narrow.

Shade began to speak again, this time his voice a little bit quieter as he leaned toward Gannon. "It is no secret any longer that my brother, the King of the Witches is missing."

Shade paused, studying Gannon's face for any kind of reaction, but he simply looked down, curled into himself out of fear. Shade continued. "It has come to my attention that there was a sighting of him in Charm City, possibly as early as yesterday. I want to know what you know."

Gannon's bottom lip began to shake, and his eyes fluttered up to Shade's and back down again. He took a step back and shook his head, no longer trying to hide how scared he was. I watched as his hand slowly reached back behind him and he shook his head. "You can't ask me to talk about things like that. I would welcome your consequences over certain people in the city."

Before I even knew what was happening, Shade's arm whipped out and a stream of magic spun around Gannon, grabbing his wrist. Shade gripped onto the rope of magic as if it were a lasso and pulled back, ripping Gannon's arm from behind him. In his hand was a dagger with a shimmering purple liquid running down the blade. Little by little, Shade pulled Gannon toward him and then tightened the rope around his wrist until the blade fell from his hand and bounced across the counter. Carefully, Shade reached down and picked it up by the handle, holding it carefully in front of him as he inspected it. He set it back down on the table and narrowed his eyes at Gannon. "Now, why would you go and do something like that?"

Gannon began to shake his head, mumbling

nervously. Shade whipped the magic again, this time wrapping the magical rope around Gannon's neck and slammed his face against the counter right in front of the blade. I stepped back, frightened by the encounter. It wasn't what I expected when Shade said I was going with him. Nonetheless, I was going to have to trust in Shade's decision-making. Eventually I would find out what that man did. Shade grabbed the dagger and stabbed it into the wooden surface, just an inch from Gannon's nose. The old man's eyes blinked wildly and I watched as the purple liquid dripped onto the desk, immediately simmering and fizzing, eating through the wood.

With his head still pressed against the counter, Gannon nodded. "Okay. Okay. I'll tell you what I know."

Shade put his hand against Gannon's head and pushed it down harder. "All of it."

Gannon nodded again, his eyes still straight ahead on the blade in front of him. He swallowed hard and then began to whisper. "I saw him walking with very large, cloaked beings through the alleyways just a few nights ago. They were in this part of the city and I was closing up for the night. I had a late-night order, but all the lights were off so I could see out the windows very easily."

Gannon stopped, but I knew just as well as Shade, that wasn't the end of it. Shade took his finger and tilted the blade of the dagger toward Gannon. The old man began to panic. "Okay. Okay. One of the men between the leader and the large, cloaked beings looked up. It was the Fae King. There was one other, but I didn't see his face. I could tell he was a captive though. His hands were held together with magical cuffs."

Shade leaned in close to him. "Is that it?"

Gannon looked at him and then over at me and shook his head. "They stopped outside the shop. They were talking outside the window not knowing I was in here. One of the men said something like, 'The King Collector is coming for all the light magic. If he has his way, it'll all be gone very soon.'"

Shade's eyes shifted up toward mine and we both knew what that meant. The King Collector was close by, and he was the one that had absolutely taken both Willa's father and most likely Shade's brother. It had been a question up to that point, but no longer. I spent my fair share of time with the King Collector, and I knew that if they were holding the Kings captive, it very well could be impossible to get them back. But not only that, things were much more dangerous than just the collecting of Kings.

It seemed the King Collector was coming for everyone.

8

Willa

I HAD NEVER BEEN to the city of the witches, as the Fae called it, but it was like being in a busy town in the Fae world.

Everything seemed quaint and sweet, but I also knew that the witches had long been over-populated with those practicing more dark magic than light. It made me pretty nervous, something I usually wasn't, to be there as not only a Fae, but a Princess. With the King missing, I would be a prime target. The last thing I wanted to do was be a prime target. Oddly, after our unceremonious greeting, I felt rather safe knowing that I had a Wizard walking around with me.

We headed into the art district. As we turned the corner, Hobbles stopped in his tracks and put his hand out, gripping my shoulder tightly. "Look at that. Have you ever seen anything more beautiful?"

I followed his stare, immediately chuckling as I found the fountain in the center of the square to be a large statue of what I could only assume was him. It was strange because the statue was erected hundreds of years before, but he stood next to me looking exactly the same age. He walked up to the fountain, looking at it dumbfounded. There were several people taking pictures of it and one lady glanced over at him, but I ignored it, or tried to. She whispered something to the man she was with and then hurried over to us.

"Excuse me," she said, tapping Hobbles on the shoulder. "I can't help but notice how much you resemble Sir Concorde. Would you mind if I took a picture of you standing in front of the fountain?"

He looked at me with rosy cheeks, huge smile, and his shoulders pulled back a little bit more, turning and posing just like the statue. Several people took pictures of him and I finally grabbed a hold of his arm and began to pull him away. "Before you become a celebrity, we're here to track down the information on my father and your King. And I really don't think you want people figuring out the truth."

He laughed with the jolliness that reminded me of the human Santa Claus. It was strange to see him that way. "Not to be a jerk, but I have to say, you seem much less asshole-ish than you did when you were in your cat form."

Still chuckling, he patted me hard on the back, and just out of his sheer size compared to mine I almost stumbled forward. "It's not pleasant when you're sharing a brain with cat instinct. While I appreciate you giving me a voice and me finding my consciousness, the days that I fought my urge to clean myself after using the litter box will forever be burned into my memory. I think you would be a little bit grumpy too."

"Yeah," I replied, cringing. "I'm really sorry about the vet appointment last week. I didn't know they took the temperature of cats like that."

He shivered so hard his whole body shook. "We're never going to speak about that again."

I nodded astutely, forcing back a smile. Hobbles began to slow and then came to a stop at a small street jetting off the main corridor of the antique shops. "I remember there being an antique shop back here that was family-run. I also remember that family not always being on the up and up. Let's see if it's still down here. I found it in my cat form of course, but I can remember some of these conversations."

As we walked slowly down the side street, I thought about what it would be like to live for 700 years as a cat. "So, did you immediately lose your consciousness when he turned you into a cat or did it take time?"

Hobbles sighed. "Unfortunately, it slowly went like a disease. At first, I was fully aware, and then over the course of about 400 years it slowly got worse and worse, and then about year 500 was when I only had small bits of information here and there that I could remember. By the time I came to you guys, there was very little left besides intuition."

I cringed. "I'm really sorry about that. And not that it makes any difference now, but I'm sorry that one of my people cut your leg off."

He stopped and looked down at me with a thoughtful gaze. "Thank you. It does mean something. No one's ever said it to me. But, thankfully because of magic, I even have feeling in my magical fake leg." We continued on for another hundred feet and then Hobbles pointed at the store door. "There it is, still alive and well I see."

For a store stuck down a long narrow alleyway, it was very well-kept. As we walked in, a small chime went off and a short man, balding on the top of his head with large aviator glasses, but not the cool sunglass kind, poked his head around the corner. He was short and thin and had a kind smile. "Welcome. Feel free to look around, and if you need any help just let me know. We also have a showroom in the back with our art pieces as well."

"Thank you," Hobbles said awkwardly.

The man didn't seem to notice. He disappeared back around the corner, and we began to peruse the shop. There were a lot of really cool things, not much different than a human antique shop. In fact, we really didn't have those kinds of things in the Fae realm. I found it fascinating how so many people enjoyed the things from the past. During those time periods, all people could do was hope and try to create better versions of those products. Now we collect them and put them on shelves.

The man that worked there was probably a long since removed ancestor of whoever originally opened the shop. He didn't seem like the kind that would be into nefarious backorder dealings, but people had surprised me in the past. I could tell by the look on Hobbles' face that he was getting the same vibe from the shop owner as I was. Still, we didn't want to be rude or draw attention to ourselves, so we continued perusing the shop up and down the rows and toward the back where the art was. As we turned the corner, the shop owner came racing toward us, his face twisted in fear, sweat peppering his forehead.

"Hide," he whispered. "They're on their way. You don't have time to get out. Hide there, behind the draperies, and no matter what happens, do not face off with them."

I furled my brow. "Sir, what can we do to help? Who are they?"

He leaned forward and whispered to both of us. "The Collector comes to take the light magic." The bells chimed at the front of the store and his eyes went wide. He hissed in a whisper pointing at the draperies, "Go, and don't come out until they're gone. No matter what happens."

I wanted to fight him, to say no and stand up to whoever he was so fearful of, but before I could say anything, Hobbles wrapped his hand over my mouth and picked me up, backing us into the long thick draperies that flowed down and across the floor. Hobbles sat me down and put his finger to his lips, shaking his head. I was irritated, but at the same time, if a big man like him, who also happened to be a very powerful Wizard was hiding, I knew I shouldn't fight him on it. Carefully I opened the draperies just enough to be able to peek through with one eye. I could see all the way down the aisle to the front of the store. The store owner was standing there, his hands clutched in front of him, nervous and shaky. Two men in black robes, their faces hidden in the shadows, stood in front of him looming down on him.

"Do you have what he wanted?"

The shop owner put his hand up and began to back away. "I told you it would take some time. I just need a little more time. I'm waiting on one person to get back to me and I'll have that information for you."

"The Collector demands the information now. Why else would we be here? Do you know what he does to people who defy him?"

A cell phone began to ring and one of the cloaked men pulled it out from his pocket, putting it up to his ear. I couldn't hear what he was saying, but the conversation was short, and when he was done, he leaned forward and whispered in the other cloaked one's ear. "Well, it seems we don't need the information after all. He has exactly what he needs, and he didn't need you to find it."

I watched as the shop owner showed a little bit of relief, but I knew that was a bad choice. I could see what was happening and I knew what was going to come of it. I wanted to do something to stop it, but as the King Collector was involved, there was nothing I could do. My powers were weak in the witch world, and I'm sure there would be some sort of blocking magic for any Fae that may tumble into the witch city.

The cloaked man doing all the talking yawned, whipping his right hand down. A ball of what looked like blue flames surrounded his hand, and the shop owner put his hands up, shaking his head. "Please. I have a family. I'll tell no one of this. My family has done many things through the years for the people that work with the Collector. They will not be happy if…"

The cloaked man shook his head and began to laugh nefariously. "Don't you understand? He has what he needs. You are of no further use to us. And he doesn't care what the others think because before long, they will bow to him too."

Before the shop owner could say anything, the

cloaked man thrust his arm out, sending a bolt of energy straight into the shop owner's chest. I clapped my hand over my mouth to stop myself from screaming as the magic lifted the shop owner off the ground and sent him flying several feet into the bookshelf behind him. Hobbles reached up and gripped my shoulder tightly, squeezing it. The two cloaked men turned and left the shop. Tears ran down my cheeks and I kept my hands clutched over my mouth, unable to move. I had never been that fearful before, or felt so helpless to help another person.

Through the window, we could see the two cloaked men as they faced each other and then disappeared, teleporting out of the witch city. I immediately threw open the drapes and ran, ignoring Hobbles yelling after me. I slid on my knees up to the shop owner who was still breathing, but blood soaked the front of his shirt. He gripped my hand tightly as he clung onto the last moments of his life. With his other hand, he reached into the pocket of his blood-soaked shirt and handed me a folded-up piece of paper. He was trying to say something, and I leaned forward, putting my ear by his mouth.

"The Fae can help. Find your father, find the Witch King, and use this to stop the Collector."

I pulled back, shocked that he had recognized me. Then again, anyone with any clout in the witch community would've known what I looked like as a child, which wasn't much different than what I looked like at that point. Just a few lines around my eyes, lines that would be growing in numbers after I got through with everything. I held the shop owner's hand as he took his last breath. I carefully set his hands on his stomach as tears ran down my cheeks and looked at the bloodstained paper in my hands.

Hobbles had been looking out the window, making sure that nobody was coming back. He ran up to me and grabbed me by the arm. "We have to leave here. We' re not safe here. They don't know who we are yet, but I've seen some very familiar faces cloaked, walking the streets right outside. We need to find Shade and Callie and get out of the city. We can talk about the paper later."

I couldn't even fight him or ask a question. Instead, I sniffled and nodded my head, taking his hand. He pulled me through the store and out the back door, looking around before we exited into the alley. I held tightly to his large hand, which completely engulfed mine, running along behind him with my tears blinding me. I gave in at that moment and I let him lead me, putting my faith in him.

After what seemed like forever, running and running, we finally stopped in another cross street, far away from the antique shop. I pressed my back to the wall, closing my eyes as I breathed in and out, trying to catch my breath. Hobbles produced a small orb, cloaking it invisible, filling it with a message for Shade, and then sent it out into the city to find him. My legs felt numb and my chest hurt, feeling the sorrow for that shop owner, for the loss of life, and for the blood that was covering my arms and hands.

Hobbles turned toward me and grabbed me by the arms, looking me straight in the eyes. "Princess, I know that was hard, but you have to pull it together. We are not out of danger yet. I think we can hide out here until Shade and Callie get to us, but I need you to not lose it right now. Can you do that for me?"

I wasn't sure if I could, but I nodded my head yes. I had never dealt with my father being missing, or my best friend being hunted, or constantly feeling fearful, something I left the whole Fae realm to get away from. But there, watching the shop owner die, especially with him knowing who I was and seeing me not help him, I could barely keep myself on my feet. Very slowly, I opened up the piece of paper and looked at it. Hobbles was staring back and forth, making sure that nobody was coming down the side street. He looked back at me. "What does it say?"

I shook my head, confused. "It's an address, but I've never heard of it before. The city is, FW, Italy."

Stopping in his tracks, Hobbles turned back and looked at me, and then down at the paper. "FW... Freedom Witches. It's a small commune kind of town, not far from here. It's hidden from the humans and it's where many of the witches who have survived helping others to safety during our wars go to live and retire and be safe. But I couldn't imagine what the King Collector would want from someone in FW. It was started by one witch whose house is in the middle of the town. They are all Freedom Fighters, not rich, not anyone who would have precious artifacts or anything like that. And there's certainly no royalty that lives in there."

I folded the piece of paper back up and stuck it in my pocket, shaking my head. "Maybe Shade will know."

There was a sound at the end of the street and my heart jumped in my chest. Hobbles slowly leaned forward, his shoulders relaxing when he found Shade and Callie hurrying down, looking for us. He waved his big hand to let them know where we were, tucked between two dumpsters. I would've thought by now the witches, with all their magic, would've found something better to do with trash. But for the moment, it was a good hiding place.

As soon as Callie saw me, I wished I had thought to get the blood off of me. Her eyes went wide, and I was surprised she didn't scream at the top of her lungs. I immediately shook my head. "It's not my blood. I'm okay."

Hobbles looked at Shade. "We were in the antique store, the old Seers family antique shop. One of their descendants was running it, a kind man, but he told us to hide and not come out. Two cloaked men came in asking him for something, but he put them off. One of them got a phone call, they said that the Collector found what he needed…"

Callie gasped. "The Collector? Like the King Collector?"

Hobbles nodded at her. "Then they killed him."

I took in a deep breath, feeling a lot braver now that Callie was there. I stepped forward and reached in my pocket, pulling out the note. "He gave this to me as he was dying. He knew who I was, and he said that the Fae could help, and that we needed to find my father and the Witch King."

Shade opened up the piece of paper and as he read, I could see a look of recognition on his face. Callie saw it too because she reached out and touched his arm. "What is it?"

"It's an address," he replied, looking perplexed. In the distance, sounds of screaming could be heard coming from the main part of the city. Shade folded the piece of paper and stuck it in his pocket, shaking his head. "We can talk about it later, we're not safe here. We have to get back. Everyone hold onto each other. I'm going to portal us out of here."

I did what Shade said and made sure that Callie had her hand in before I put mine in as well. As I reached for it, two voices yelled out from the end of the street. "It's them! Don't let them leave, the Collector wants them!"

Shade looked back at me and nodded. I shoved my hand forward, throwing it on top of his. We portalled back to the witch mansion, landing softly in the grass. I felt numb, and though I wanted to cry more, I couldn't. I just wanted to take a shower and get the blood off of me. Hobbles walked over and helped me to my feet, and I smiled kindly at him. Shade pulled the paper back out and we stood, the four of us staring down at it.

"This is an address, and I know this address," Shade said. "But it doesn't make any sense. My great, great, great aunt was one of the Freedom Fighters a long time ago. Before that, she was kind of like a witch version of Indiana Jones. She liked to travel and find old relics of things. There's a stone cold the Finder Stone. There were five people that found it, and when broken up into pieces and consumed on a yearly basis, it will prolong your life until you run out. They split the stone, and last year, her stones ran out. This is the address to her house. But I can't possibly even begin to believe that my aunt had anything the King Collector would want. She was like the witch version of the hippies from the 60s, old, liked to do crafts, and think about the amazing things she did in her life. But she wasn't rich, and she didn't keep keepsakes."

Callie put her arm around me and held me tightly against her. "Well, whatever the King Collector's looking for, or whatever he found, he found it at your aunt's house. The only way to know is to go there. The shop owner did us a favor, and he protected the witches and the Fae, but he gave his life to do it."

I sat up, wiping the tear from my cheek. "Callie's right. He gave his life for all of us. We owe it to him. We go there tonight. We find this King Collector, and we take him down no matter what it takes."

9

Callie

"I TOTALLY UNDERSTAND why you'd want to go out right now. I get it. You watched something really terrible happen, and you're terrified that something is going to happen to your father. But we don't know what we'll find at this house. We don't even know what we're looking for. With your powers being subdued here, and mine being unreliable, at best, I just think that we should wait until daytime to go out to the house and check it out." I was trying to talk some sense into Willa.

Talking sense into Willa was not something I

was used to doing. In fact, I didn't think I had ever done it before in our entire friendship. She had always been the one to talk me off the ledge. It was completely reasonable, and I understood. At the same time though, if we went barreling into this house and there were a thousand dark entities waiting for us, we wouldn't get very much accomplished.

Instead, I wanted Willa to rest, to get herself together, and for all of us to be safe when we went. I knew I was asking a lot from her. When my parents died, if I had been given a time machine to go back, even if it meant I could die, no one would've been able to talk me out of it. But at the same time, her father wasn't dead, not that we knew of. The King Collector wanted us, and he knew we were hunting him. The last thing we wanted to do was walk straight into his grasp.

Willa stood up from her bed and I watched as she took a deep breath and began to pace slowly back and forth in front of me. I noticed the little things that she had never done before, the way she folded her hands in front of her and fiddled with her fingers. She wasn't the girl that really had nervous habits. She was the girl that had more common sense than anybody I knew.

"I know you're right," she finally said with an

exhaustive sigh. "It's exactly what I would tell you. In fact, I would tell you that you were insane for even thinking of going out tonight after the day we've had. But I also know you can empathize with how I'm feeling right now."

I stood up and wrapped my arms around Willa. "Of course I can. But if you go tonight, just know, I am coming with you. That means Hobbles and Shade are coming too."

Willa pulled back and her mouth dropped open. She let out a deep dramatic gasp. "That's tricky. That's downright maniacal. You know darn well I wouldn't put your lives at risk for anything. Maybe I was wrong, maybe all this adventuring isn't good for you after all."

I laughed and hugged her again. "I learned from the best."

We both chuckled and looked at each other suspiciously before laughing again. A loud knock sounded on the door, making us both jump. Willa shook her head as she walked to the door to open it. "We need to get it together."

"I've been telling myself that for the last forty years," I replied.

It felt good to laugh. I felt like it had been forever since we really genuinely enjoyed a moment. Everything was always so stressful, and I understood why, but I still wasn't used to it. I went from shy, withdrawn, and safe to full on magical being, hunting down the most dangerous villains in all the realms. Hell, I was like a fantasy novel come to life.

When Willa opened the door, Shade was standing on the other side, leaned against the doorframe with a smirk on his face. "I came to tell you guys dinner was ready, but all I could hear was cackling."

Willa narrowed her eyes. "Then you should be used to it since you're a witch."

She walked straight past him and I held back a laugh, patting him on the chest as I followed. "All we need now are brooms and we'll be able to get around."

Shade groaned and closed Willa's door before turning and following us quickly down the hallway. I knew where I was going, and Willa seemed to know, but I had a feeling she was just dramatically walking off. Shade hurried in front of us, and Willa gave me a sly smile and a wink of her eye. We entered the formal dining room, and it felt a lot emptier than it had when I was there before. He kept us in the formal dining room, and I had a feeling it was because of both Sir Concorde a.k.a. Hobbles, and because technically, Willa was royalty just like Shade. Actually, Willa was, or should have been the future Queen of the Fae while Shade was the brother to the King. I suppose that made him a prince, but I wasn't sure how the whole witch world did things.

Inside the dining hall was a large, long wooden table, with high back chairs all around it, and Hobbles sitting at one end. Food was spread out across the surface and I hadn't even realized how hungry I was until we walked inside. It wasn't like the Fae world where during my first dinner, I was totally confused on what to eat. This was normal human food and it smelled delicious.

I sat next to Willa and across from Shade as we dug in. Everyone was very quiet during dinner, and I wasn't sure whether it was because of what had happened that day, or because everyone was just that hungry. The only one that wasn't quiet was Hobbles, who seemed to groan after every single bite of food. It hadn't dawned on me until dinner that up until that point, Hobbles had only been eating cat food and tuna. He hadn't had a good human meal in over 700 years. None of us said anything about it, actually finding it kind of amusing. I just liked the fact that it lightened up the mood in the room.

The witch castle was beautiful, but it was very dark, and when someone had already had a rough day, there wasn't much light to brighten things up. By the time dinner was over, Willa was yawning, and I could see in her eyes that she was ready for bed. Before the desert had even been brought out, Willa had already kissed me on the top of the head, nodded to the two others, and headed off to bed early. Honestly, I thought it was the best thing for her. She had a very hard day and no one blamed her for wanting some time alone. In fact, with what the next day had in store, it was probably a good idea if all of us went to bed.

Hobbles leaned back in his chair and rubbed his stomach. "That was delicious, Shade. Thank you."

Shade nodded, and I could see he was holding back a proud smile. "Absolutely. It's nice to actually have somebody to cook for besides me. I had told them to stop and I would go to the cafeteria with everybody else, but with guests in the house, we decided to go all out."

Hobbles' eyes roamed around the room, looking at the tapestries and the large paintings hanging on the walls. I followed his eyes around the room and realized I had never taken a really good look at what was decorating the place.

Above each of the paintings were weapons with small plaques that I couldn't read. Hobbles nodded at one, an old gentleman, his eyes dark, wearing robes not that much different than the ones we had worn in the city earlier. "Arthur Shadow, one of the greatest warriors that I had the pleasure of knowing during the Great War."

Shade looked over his shoulder. "My great, great, great uncle. I've heard a lot of stories about him, but most of them have not been about him on the battlefield, if you know what I mean. Though there are some very epic tales."

Hobbles began to laugh again, this one deep from his belly. "That reminds me of one night. It's not a funny story, but it does show your uncle's ability to lead and inspire. It was about midway through the war and I wasn't yet a leader. I remember it was one of the bloodier battles, lots of men died. The battle ended somewhere around dawn, and we spent all day gathering our dead. The Great War didn't have a minimum age to fight. There were boys, as young as thirteen fighting in the war. Whoever had control over their magical abilities was suited up and sent out. Some of those boys never made it to be men. In fact, most of them did not. That was the hardest part about collecting our dead. When you picked up a young child's body, magic still simmering on their fingertips, it took a piece of you."

His voice was somber, and neither Shade nor I said anything. We gave him the space and the respect that both of us felt was appropriate in that moment. Sure, the witches weren't my people, but war was war. And children were children.

After a few moments, staring off in the distance, Hobbles blinked his eyes and continued with the story. "We always made it a point after a day like that to have a celebration of sorts. None of us really knew what we were celebrating, but it felt good to drink and laugh, and listen to jokes. Later in the night, when the moon was high, and the majority of the men were passed out somewhere, the mood got solemn again. It was a full moon, and when you looked out over the field you could see all of the bodies draped in cloth, waiting for the ceremony."

I rubbed my arms, chills running up and down them.

Hobbles glanced at me but didn't say a word. He gave a moment of thought to his last sentence and then continued. "Your great, great, great uncle, three sheets to the wind, carrying a jug of ale, decided to pay tribute to the men. If anybody had walked up at that moment, they would've never known he had a drop of alcohol in his system. He lit up the sky with magic, the same kind that's used at the witch's mourning ceremonies after a death." Hobbles looked over at me to explain. "It looks like the aurora borealis, only much more vibrant, colorful, and beautiful. Normally, that kind of show will have a personal touch. The colors would represent the dead, but since there were so many, it was like a rainbow in the sky."

"That sounds beautiful," I replied.

"Anyway, as the light shimmered through the sky, he began to sing an old song, sung by his grandfather during the war before that. It was a tribute to the dead, a look toward a brighter future, but a sad song, nonetheless. His voice echoed for miles. We were sure that the enemy could hear it, but none of us were fearful that they would come. They knew where we were, and the one thing about the Great War was, when the battle was over, neither side would begin a new battle until all respects were paid to the dead. It was the only civil thing about the war. I'm not even sure it was an order from the dark mage, but the men fighting on the outside understood the unspoken rule."

Hobbles picked up his cup of wine and chugged it, wiping the dribble off his chin before continuing. "Afterward, he made this big speech and all the men were ready for the next day and rejuvenated. It was pretty amazing to watch. I'm sad to know that he's no longer here. Or at least I'm assuming that since his picture's on the wall."

Shade gave him a half smile and shook his head. "He died long before I was ever born. My father told me that when he came back from the war, he was a different man, a different witch. He went into hiding, stayed mostly to himself, and didn't fight for a longer life or to stay healthy. He drank and smoked, and unlike the Fae, our bodies are very human. We may live longer, but we have to take care of ourselves."

Hobbles nodded knowingly, and I wondered if during his time roaming the Earth he ever felt that way. I had never been to war, but I had felt like hiding away for the rest of my life, not facing the things going on in my life. I wasn't sure I would even survive something like the Great War, no matter how powerful I was, I didn't have the personality to do it.

Sensing the tension, Hobbles took in a deep breath and clapped his hands as they walked in with dessert. I chuckled and shook my head at the staff. Laying my napkin on the plate, I pushed the chair back and stood up. "While I appreciate everything, Shade, Hobbles, I think it's time for me to go to bed. We have a big day tomorrow, and who knows what it'll bring. I'll see you guys at breakfast?"

Hobbles had already started eating his dessert and just shook his head with a mouthful. Shade stood up. "Do you want me to walk you back?"

I shook my head. "No, thank you. I might go for a small walk outside around the castle first, just to clear my head. You guys enjoy your evening. I'll see you in the morning."

10

Callie

I LEFT THE DINING HALL, but the entire time I was walking across to the door and out, I could feel Shade watching me.

The truth was, I did want him to walk me back, but I didn't want to be the one to make that choice. He had been there for me all day long, on multiple occasions, and I needed to remember that he was going through something tough too. I wasn't going to put my expectations on him, or my disappointment.

I headed through the house, out the front

doors, down the steps, and out into the yard without skipping a beat. I chuckled as I walked along, heading toward the edge of the house and around the side toward the gardens. It wasn't that long ago that I had first come out of the house after being kidnapped, running straight for the front gate. I could still feel the pain from slamming into that invisible barrier. I think it was more pain of my pride than anything else. That was before I even knew the bracelet had any effect on me at all. In fact, I was pretty confused about everything at that point. It all seemed different though, now that I understood magic and what was real and what wasn't.

As I reached the edge of the garden, I sat down on the stone bench at the entrance and looked up at the clear night sky. It was clearer and more beautiful than I had ever seen before. The stars sparkled and shimmered, and I saw several shooting stars within thirty seconds of sitting down. Back at home, we never got to see the sky like that.

"You're not trying to figure out how to destroy my magical boundary again are you?"

I looked over my shoulder, finding Shade standing there, his arms crossed, a smirk on his face. I scooted over on the bench and patted it, coaxing him to sit next to me. He hesitated for a moment but then came over and sat down. I shook my head, looking at the bracelet. "I still don't know how I did that. How does it make you feel?"

He lifted a brow. "How does what make me feel? You constantly being in danger? Not great."

I shook my head. "No, knowing that a puny little human, with somebody else's magical bracelet, broke your big bad protection spell."

He lifted his chin defiantly. "It was beginner's luck. Besides, everything that happened led to this moment here, and the moments we've had in the last few days. It may just lead us forward in stopping the King Collector and returning my brother and Willa's father to their thrones. So, I guess I'm not too upset about it."

Shade gave me a boyish grin and I felt butterflies flutter in my stomach. Sitting on that small bench, we were touching shoulders, hips, and legs. It felt natural though, not forced or awkward, but like we had done it for a very long time. I kind of expected him to come outside to find me, not necessarily to spend time with me, but just to make sure that I was safe. What I didn't expect was his hand sliding from his lap over and taking mine. I looked down at it as he wrapped my hand in his, realizing just how small I was compared to him. And I wasn't necessarily physically that much smaller, but the humans, we were definitely different and more fragile than even the witches who were, for all intents and purposes, humans with magic.

I wanted to lean into him, for him to wrap his arms around me and tell me everything would be okay, but I knew that was not really in the cards. Even if it could be, even if that were why he was there, I wasn't ready for that kind of heartbreak. It was hard enough for me to stay concentrated on a daily basis with everything so out of control, but to add negative emotions to that, it might just get me killed. Still, I didn't pull away. I didn't for anything in the world want to offend him.

We sat there in silence for several moments, just staring up at the sky. When he got up, he turned toward me and pulled me to my feet. But he didn't stop there, he pulled me right into him and our noses touched before our eyes latched on to one another. I could tell he didn't mean to do it, but I could also tell he didn't want to pull away. His hands slid from mine and reached up, cupping my face. I closed my eyes as he leaned in, feeling his lips gently grazing each of my eyes, the tip of my nose, and then my lips.

I let out a small coo as he pressed his lips harder against mine, letting one of his hands drop to my hip, and the other grip the back of my neck. My fingers pressed against his chest, and I knew I couldn't fight it even if I wanted to. All the chemistry and tension that had built up since I met him came flooding out in that passionate embrace. I felt weightless, as if my feet would lift from the ground at any moment. It was the perfect kiss, one that I never wanted to end.

But as the sound of voices in the distance rang out, signaling it was the change of station for the guards, Shade quickly pulled back. He looked longingly into my eyes for several moments and then tore his gaze away, releasing his hands from me, and stepping back. "I'm sorry. I shouldn't have..."

"Why not?" I asked him brazenly. "What's so wrong with it?"

His eyes met mine once again. "Nothing. There's nothing wrong with it. But...it's just...I can't..."

Silence fell between us for a few agonizing minutes and then he sighed and leaned forward, kissing me on the forehead before walking away. Everything in me wanted to call out for him, but I knew it wouldn't change anything. I knew that whatever the reason he was racing off like the house was on fire, it wasn't going to change just because I expressed to him my want. I was too exhausted for any of it. I just wanted to go upstairs, lay down in my bed, and fall asleep. Maybe the next day would be better than the one I just had.

It had to be, right?

11

Callie

I WAS FOOLING myself thinking that I could actually go to sleep and have a good restful night.

I couldn't remember the last time that I had a good night's sleep. I thought for sure though, being in the middle of everything, my dreams would subside a bit. Maybe it was the magic in the Fae realm that made me sleep so well. As much as I liked the world of the witches, it was not doing me any good at all. My dream this time though, it was different.

My eyes opened and I found myself inside the

cave, but I was not in a dream like state. The dreams up until that point had been me and my body, but my consciousness was just kind of along for the ride and my dream-self did whatever it wanted to do. This time though, I was awake in my dream. I looked around me, reaching out and touching the wall. I rubbed my fingertips together, feeling the wetness, and my arms felt the chill of the cold air. It reminded me of going to the caverns with my parents when I was a kid.

Ahead of me was the archway, and even though I knew what was beyond it, it seemed normal. It seemed like anything you would find spelunking or exploring. But I knew it was more than that. I knew what was waiting for me on the other side. Well, at least I kind of knew. I started to walk forward, but the sound of a familiar voice echoed in my ears. I turned and looked over my shoulder, finding Shade with his arm out as if he were calling after me, but I hadn't gone anywhere.

This is so weird.

It seemed that even though I knew I was dreaming, Shade was still in that reenactment stage, so I turned away from him and ran straight toward the archway just like I did in my dream.

When I stepped through and came to a skipping stop, there I was in the eerie gray place where I always ended up. I watched as the spirits swirled around, the voices echoing, and the overwhelming feeling of being alone, but obviously not really alone, overwhelmed me. I turned back toward the doorway, but it was gone as usual.

That's when things really started to change. Instead of hearing footsteps behind me, a cold wind whipped around me, like stepping into an air-conditioned room after being outside on a 100° day. I wrapped my arms around myself and shivered.

Looking down at my arm, I noticed a mark, and as I uncrossed them, the mark turned into a handprint. It was exactly where the frozen hand had touched me. But that frozen hand had never been in my dream before.

"Great, now I'm just combining all of my worst fears," I sighed.

"Not all of them," a deep and familiar voice said from behind me.

Everything inside of me, every bone, every muscle, and even my heart stopped right then and there. Very slowly, I turned around, ready to face the King Collector. However, just like before, just like when I was taken in Rome, he refused to show his face. Instead, floating all around me were his large caped creatures. My bracelet tingled wildly on my arm and I reached over, cupping it with my hand.

"Something pretty for my collection," the King Collector whispered.

Just as anger began to boil inside of me, it was overrun by the sheer amount of fear I felt as all of the tall, cloaked figures stopped and turned toward me, synchronized, staring at me from the black abyss within their hoods. I un-cupped my bracelet and took a step backward, fumbling with my footing on the stones beneath my feet. "Wake up, Callie." I was speaking through gritted teeth, and I really needed myself to wake up. I stepped back again, but they just kept coming for me.

Without thinking, I turned and attempted to make a run for it, not really sure where I could go, considering everything seemed to be nothing but a dead gray flat surface in all directions. But, as soon as I picked up my foot, the spirits wrapped around my legs and held me down in place. I shuffled back around to face the dark entities, figuring maybe I wasn't in a dream. Maybe that was how it all ended. As they raced toward me, a loud booming sound echoed out, and the ripples could be seen all through the air, moving toward me. The dark entities turned in all directions watching it close in on us.

I braced myself for impact, but when it hit, it didn't touch me. It went right through me. I opened my eyes and glanced back and forth, finding that the impact pushed back all of the dark entities. It didn't give me much time to escape, but it was enough for someone else to slip in between and grab me by the shoulders. It was Hobbles, in his full-grown form, but with his cat head. It startled me, and I pushed him back. "What in the hell..."

"Callie! Wake up! Wake up now!" With that, he held his hand in front of me, fur growing from the back of it, and snapped his fingers loudly.

My eyes shot wide open and I sat straight up in the bed, gasping for air. I looked around me, finding Hobbles standing next to the bed with his hand on my shoulder, a look of worry on his face. "Callie, thank the wizards. I've been trying to wake you this whole time."

I looked at him, confused. "How did you know I was in a dream?"

Suddenly, the castle all around us shook, and there was a loud boom. Voices yelled out from outside and I could hear hundreds of footsteps, like soldiers marching. "What was that?"

"The dark witches are here, and they want you. They want you, and Willa, and Shade. We've got to get you out of here."

"What?" I asked, shaking my head as I jumped out of the bed. "I have to help them. I'm not going anywhere."

"Oh yes you are," Willa said as she rushed into the room. "There's no way we can stand against them. We will only get in the witches' ways. I just gotta figure out a clean and clear way to get you out of here. To get all of us out here. Hobbles, can you teleport?"

Hobbles lifted both eyebrows. "Well, it's been a very long time, and it was a little bit different back then, but I think I can get us from point A to point B in one piece."

"You think?" I replied, not at all sure about taking whatever teleportation manner that Hobbles had practiced some 700 years before. "I think that it's pretty reasonable to expect that we wouldn't be too happy about not knowing if we were going to end up back at our house in sixteen different pieces or fused together as one."

Shade rushed into the room and shut the door behind him. More loud booms echoed outside and the castle shook again. "No need to teleport. There's a passageway." He walked across my room, over to the fireplace, and ran his fingers along the seams of the stone walls. When he came to a stop, he used his magic and pulled one of the stones out. Inside was a lever. He pulled the lever and a doorway leading to a staircase opened out of thin air. It wasn't on the wall, on the floor, or even behind the fireplace. It was literally out of thin air, which made me wonder why in the world they needed a lever.

I would have to ask the questions later though. Willa hurried through the door, turned, and stopped, waiting for us. I shook my head. "No. You fought for us, and we need to fight for you."

Shade smiled at me. "And you have, and you will in the future. But this is my home, and our troops will fight them off. You have the bracelet, and Willa is the Princess. Both of you need to get out of here just in case."

Willa reached out and grabbed my arm, pulling me. I fought her for a second just looking into Shade's eyes, and then gave in, stepping inside, waiting for Hobbles. He stood in front of Shade and they gripped each other's elbows, paying respects. Hobbles shook his head. "I feel like I should stay here and fight."

Shade put his other hand on Hobbles' shoulder. "There will be plenty of fighting. The most important thing is that Callie and Willa make it out of here safely. The tunnel will lead into the city, Rome, not the witch city. It was the tunnel built during the Great War and was originally going to be used as a crypt, but then they built this house over it because no bodies were ever buried there."

Hobbles looked at him knowingly. "I remember that. I helped build that. I was wondering if it was still here. I can come back if you need me, just send a sign."

I stepped forward, putting my hand on the magical door. "Shade, will you meet us when you're finished?"

His eyes shifted to Willa and then back to me as if I couldn't read between the lines. The likelihood of them winning that fight without more magic was slim to none. And from the sounds of it, and the mass of magic going on outside, the dark witches had amassed, and I had a feeling the castle was the only place they were attacking. Shade forced a smile as if I couldn't see through it, but it didn't make me angry. I appreciated him attempting to calm my fear. "We will see each other soon. Now go, the storekeeper at the other end of this tunnel will know what to do."

I stood there, watching as Shade shut the door. When it closed it disappeared, leaving us on the firelit stairwell. I couldn't get over the fact that my heart hurt at the situation. I didn't feel that it was right to just walk away from them. We continued down the stairs, and Hobbles grabbed one of the torches off the wall, holding it up as we walked through. Hobbles was much larger than I realized he was, and looked even bigger in that small space. His head was close to the ceiling and his shoulders nearly touched each side.

Dust and pebbles fell from the ceiling as another loud boom echoed above us and I could only imagine what it looked like up there. It just wasn't right. Something just did not feel right.

"Stop."

Both Willa and Hobbles stopped and turned back, looking at me curiously. I shook my head. "If this were happening to our home, would the witches run away from us? Shade is just as important as any of us. In fact, every single witch out there is just important as any of us. I know that you guys have a deep history in royalty, but that's not how we do things, at least not in California. Everybody's worth is the same. Shade and his people have gone above and beyond to help us and protect us. I have the bracelet, Hobbles is a

Grand Master Wizard, witch mage, or whatever, and you're Willa, and with or without magic I wouldn't want to fight you."

Willa stared at me for several seconds and then up at Hobbles who shook his head. "You're the Princess. You have to make the decision."

"There's something about that bracelet that is particularly important to the Collector. It goes beyond trying to get me. If we go back there, he could take you."

I nodded "I know. And he could kill me."

Willa shook her head and stepped forward, the light of the fire flickering against her face. "He could do much more than that. Death would be a relief."

I clenched my teeth, pushing down the fear. Shade's face, the other witches, the city, the Fae, Hobbles, everyone, they all went through my head at that moment, and I knew that if we ran, we could not stand in solidarity with anyone else. "I can't leave. We have to help."

Willa's eyes glistened, and her mouth curved just enough to look like she was smiling at me. She looked back at Hobbles and gave him a grin. He shook his head. "And to think, before all this happened, I thought you would one day die a crazy old cat lady, and my brothers and sisters would eat you."

I covered my mouth, and Willa burst into laughter. Another boom rattled the tunnel. Willa gave a stout nod. "Let's go help them. But when you get up there, you have to let the magic free."

I took a deep breath. "That's the plan, but I'll be honest, I have no idea what I'm doing."

12

Shade

I STOOD IN THE COURTYARD, watching as the dark witches and beings lined up, appearing one after the other after the other.

I had only ever heard about that many in one place in stories of the Great War. They had been gathering under everybody's noses and I was so preoccupied in finding my brother that I hadn't even realized it. Callie was safe, Willa was safe, and Hobbles was with them, so I put that out of my mind. I knew when I sent them on their way that it may be the last time that I saw them, but that made my decision to walk away from Callie the night before even more important.

To my right, the light the dark were battling, and to my left the dark were winning. In front of me, dark witches came racing toward us, using their magic as weapons. They launched on us, creating swords and clubs with magic, and attacking with creatures I had never seen before. A javelin of dark magic came whirling through the air straight at me and I ducked to the left, barely avoiding it.

From my right, a creature came barreling at me, human in size, but with gray spiky fur coming from his neck, and fangs that dripped a green liquid down each corner of his mouth. I swung my arms through the air and blasted him with magic to the chest, sending him flipping backward, head over feet, and landing on the ground with a thud.

One of my witches was being attacked by several creatures at the same time, but that was happening all around me. I didn't know what to do. I didn't know where to focus my energy. I thrust both arms out in the air and just started sending magic flying, focusing its intent on the darkness. I hoped that in some way I could help my fellow witches, while also keeping myself alive. If I fell, there was no royal line left, and nothing to protect anyone anymore.

The gate had been blown wide open, shards of twisted metal lay on the ground, and the dome of protection that had been placed was nothing but dissipated magic on the ground. In the distance, I could see more and more witches appearing, jumping from their portals at a full speed run, heading straight toward us. It seemed they would never stop coming. Smoke billowed from one of the smaller houses on the compound, and magical fire crackled and burned from the explosions.

I pushed up my sleeves and took a deep breath. If we were going to go down, I was going to fight with everything that I had. If they won that battle, hopefully our actions would inspire others to fight the war. And I hoped that whatever I did for Willa and Callie helped them because they may be the only chance we had at a future.

13

Callie

WHEN WE REACHED the top of the steps we had just come down, I found myself facing a solid stone wall and realized that we had come through a magical doorway. That magical doorway hadn't been opened by a spell or show of sparkling energy. Shade had pulled the lever.

A lever...

I looked all over the wall, ran my hands over the stone, and searched every corner of that small space. Willa and Hobbles did the same up the walls behind me, but there was no lever. I replayed Shade's motion in my head, burned into my memory because just moments before I thought it would be the last time that I ever saw him. It dawned on me, the lever wasn't out in the open. It was hidden behind a stone that was taken out by magic.

Right when the thought crossed my mind, my bracelet began to tingle and I lifted my hand, letting the magic guide me. I was focused, fully focused on what was in front of me. It felt as if the magic was pulling me forward until my hand landed on the center stone. I took my finger and traced around the edges, watching as magic left a line like a pencil behind my finger. When it came back around and connected, the stone cracked and then burst into small pieces, falling to the ground.

The magic released and I hurried forward, pulling all the small stones out of the hole until nothing was left but the identical lever. I pulled the lever and turned around, watching the door appear. Willa smirked. "You're getting the hang of it."

"I hope I'll learn a little bit faster," I said as the tunnel rumbled again from above.

The three of us raced through the doorway, into my room, and then out into the hallway. We weren't sure what we would find, but it seemed that the dark magic witches hadn't made their way into the house yet. The halls were vacant and flashes of light radiated from the windows. We ran over and stopped, staring out at the scene below.

For the first time since Hobbles had turned into a human, I saw a completely exasperated look on his face. "Good God. They've amassed again."

I could see Shade down there, standing between bodies, fighting with everything he had. I gripped onto Hobbles' arm and looked up at him. "Come on. We are not going to be afraid of a fight today."

Hobbles grinned. "Damn right."

Willa cracked her knuckles, the little bit of a magic that she could use trickling down her arms. "I'm not too good to punch somebody in the nose."

We ran down the hallway, taking the twists and turns until we found ourselves at the side entrance of the house. There was too much fighting at the front for us to get through, so we figured if we came around the side, maybe we could be of help, at least a little bit. The witches with Shade were outnumbered 5 to 1, and the dark magic was strong. I knew that from ex-perience.

Outside, we walked side-by-side, marching around the building to face the fighting. As we appeared, a large gnarly looking beast came racing toward Hobbles. He stayed calm until the last second and then turned, his muscles bulging, and roared as he lifted the creature into the air and then slammed him down on his knee, throwing him to the side. Three witches came running at us with weapons that looked to be made directly from their magic. The one on the right facing Hobbles had a club with spikes, the one on the left a bow and arrow, and the one heading straight for me with a maniacal smile on his face held two daggers, one in each hand.

I had never, in my entire life, been trained in hand-to-hand combat, but for some reason, in that moment, that did not even cross my mind. I could feel the energy from the bracelet coursing through my entire body. It palpitated through my veins, and I could feel it moving across my skin. Hobbles went one way, Willa went the other, and I ran straight forward, my eyes locked on the evil bastard that was obviously hell-bent on taking me down. It was also obvious he didn't know who I was because I knew, without a doubt, the

King Collector wanted me, but he wanted me alive.

"Okay magic, it's time to do your thing," I whispered to myself, releasing those walls that I'd held so tightly to since the bracelet had been put on me.

As I did, it was like a floodgate.

The witch lunged at me, one dagger in the air and the other at his waist. As he came down, I stood there, my body calm until he was close enough for me to reach him. The magic moved me, and my left arm raised, grabbing him by the wrist while the other knocked the magical dagger from his hand. It slammed into the ground and dissipated into a mist. His eyes went wide as he stared at me, unsure of where I was getting that kind of strength. It was obviously not from my forty-year-old, weak as hell arms. But it was definitely from the magic.

Still, the witch buckled in and pushed harder, trying to drive the dagger into my shoulder. With his other hand, he gripped me around the throat, but I didn't flinch. It was as if the magic was keeping all of my emotions away. There was no fear, there was no sadness, or panic. I was calm and collected and I could think clearer than I ever had before. It was as if the magic had swept away all the noise in my head and created a pathway and open space to think clearly.

As his fingers pressed against my neck and mine against his wrist, his magic began to seep down my arms and toward my bracelet. I watched as it entered the bracelet, and then came back out, thicker, fuller, and with a speed I couldn't even explain. It rocketed out of the jewelry and slammed straight into the witch, twisting around him until he couldn't move.

The witch's hand released from my throat, and the dagger fell from his other hand. I stepped back, watching him as he struggled, and then flicked my wrist, sending him flying through the air. The magic pulled back inside of me and lowered just a bit. I was glad because the hum of it in my ears was so loud I could barely hear anything else.

"Callie," Willa said, excitement in her eyes. "I know what the bracelet's doing. I know what it's doing and I think we can use that. We can use it on everyone. Do you trust me?"

I rolled my eyes at her, my arm flinging out and knocking a witch right in the face, his nose breaking beneath my palm. I looked over at him, slightly alarmed as he groaned and fell into a heap on the ground. "I fully trust you, of course.

Though, to be completely transparent here, the magic is kind of ruling me right now."

Willa nodded and grabbed my other arm, pulling me out into the center of the battle. "That's okay. My magic is in that bracelet too. Like I said, I don't know for sure this'll work but from what I know of the bracelet, which is not a lot, it ultimately uses whatever magic is being used against it. But it also stores that as well. There's probably more to it than that, but I think that if we use what little power I have and couple it with the bracelet..."

I bit the inside of my cheek and looked around, finding Shade in the crowd. His eyes lifted to mine, and he looked absolutely mortified to see me. Still, he couldn't come to me, he was too busy fighting for his life. Blood trickled down his forehead, and I could see the exhaustion in his body. I looked back at Willa. "Kaplooey."

She tilted her head to the side. "What?"

I made the hand gesture of an explosion, mimicking the sounds with my mouth. "You know, take them all out at once."

"I like how you think. Go big or go home?"

I glanced around one last time. "I think at this point, it's go big or die."

Callie and I both took a deep breath, not

knowing if it would work, and if it did, what it would do to either of us. I reached out my hand and clasped hers, and almost instantly, a flash of energy slammed into both of us. I could feel her energy moving through her and into me and back around like a circuit. I could feel every movement of it, and it was incredibly intense.

I glanced over at her. "Remember! Focus on the dark magic. We don't want to kill everyone."

She gave me a nod, her eyes watering from the intensity of our connection. We both turned back, closed our eyes, and tilted our heads back. I could feel us both release the tension holding back the fullness of the magic at the same time. It was the wildest of feelings. It was hard to keep my mind focused on dark magic, but I knew the people's lives depended on it. Our lives depended on it. I felt the rush hit us from the tops of our heads down through our bodies and then it slammed into the ground. I could feel the shaking of the earth beneath our feet and the sound of magical explosions came to a stop.

The way that the magic rushed through us wasn't painful, but felt like we were standing in a wind tunnel, only the wind was slamming straight down on the top of our heads. I managed to pry my eyes open, watching as a wave of translucent magic, a ring of intensity, spread out from our feet. Those closest to us immediately flew back, and like dominoes, it continued outward, on and on. In the distance, nothing but black robes racing forward could be seen. But when the ring of energy hit them, they fell, and they fell hard. I wasn't sure why, but the energy affected different beings in different ways. Many were knocked unconscious, but others, like the snarling human sized beasts, burst into dust and blew off with the wind.

As the energy blew through us, exiting out into a wake of destruction for the dark magic witches, Willa and I released hands. For a moment, I felt energized and wildly awake, but then it hit me like a ton of bricks. It felt like I had used every bit of energy that I'd ever had in my life. My knees buckled, and I fell to the ground. I turned my head and looked over, finding that Willa had done the same. We were both breathing heavily, but the adrenaline and the fear of what was to come slipped away, and Willa began to laugh wildly. Her laughter was contagious, and I sat back on my butt, shaking my head.

"Did you see that?" Willa squealed. "That was amazing!"

"Amazingly exhausting. I feel more tired than

that one time in third grade when I got mono after drinking fruit juice from the same Sippy boxes as my best friend."

Willa wrinkled her nose. "Never share Sippy boxes."

I tapped my nose and pointed at her. "I'll remember that for the future. Thanks."

All around us, witches began to stand up, and they weren't the dark ones either. Shade made his way through the crowd that was beginning to gather around Willa and me, and put his hand down, helping me to my feet. He turned and did the same for Willa who nodded and smiled at the ones who were thanking her. Shade shook his head at me. "You shouldn't have come back."

I blinked at him. "But then... You'd still be fighting."

I smirked at him and he rolled his eyes. We both looked around, watching as many of the dark witches began to wake up and then immediately disappear into their portals. Shade looked back and forth and through the crowd. "Where's Hobbles? I mean, Sir Concorde."

My smile quickly faded, realizing that I didn't even think for five seconds about all the injured people around me. My heart fluttered nervously in my chest as I scanned the crowd, knowing that it shouldn't be hard to find Hobbles, he was about a foot taller and three feet wider than everybody else. I reached out and tapped Willa. "Hobbles... Do you see him?"

Willa's smile faded too, and she began to look around frantically. I hadn't realized until that moment just how close she had gotten to him after the incident in the town the day before. We split up in all directions, moving carefully through the grass, respectfully stepping over anyone that had fallen during the battle. Up ahead, I could see a pile of beasts, their bodies twisted and mangled as if they had been broken. I walked around them, hearing a groan.

Sitting, his back to the bodies as if they were nothing more than a pile of rocks, clutching a bleeding wound on his stomach, was Hobbles. I looked up toward the crowd and waved my arms at Shade and Willa before dropping to my knees next to him. "Hobbles, what do I do? I think there's a healer here." I looked up from him as Willa and Shade slowed their pace, seeing the damage. "Get the healer! Someone get the healer!"

Hobbles reached up and touched my arm, giving me the best smile that he could, despite his mouth full of blood. "It's okay human. I seem to have stumbled on someone's sword. You know, after 700 years of thinking that I would die one day as roadkill, I'd have to say going out this way would be a bit better."

I shook my head, tears immediately filling my eyes. "No! Don't talk like that. You did not survive 700 years to bail on us now."

Willa stepped up and put her hand on my shoulder, softly saying my name. I looked back at her, and I could see the look on her face. I knew what that look meant. I had seen that look one other time in my life. I saw it when I went to the hospital to find out if my parents were okay after their car accident. The nurse was trying to tell me that they had died, but I couldn't comprehend. One of my father's friends who I had grown up with had stepped up behind me, put his hand on my shoulder just like Willa, said my name just like Willa did, and gave me the same look that Willa had. It was a look of pity. It was a look of reality. But I wasn't ready to accept reality.

I shook my head. "No. You have all this magic, beasts with snarling teeth, dark witches, light witches, mages, Fae, weird skeleton creatures with cold hands, but you can't heal a wound? It's bullshit."

Hobbles' hand came up and touched my cheek and I turned back to him, putting my hand in his and holding it tightly. "I've watched you go from a scared human to a bad ass in a very short amount of time. You were the best human I ever had. I know that you can save them, but in order to save them you have to let people go too. You can't save everyone." He coughed, and his words began to slow as his eyelids drooped. "You're their hope and I know you can... Do... Anything. Thank you... For everything."

Hobbles' eyes shut and his hand slipped from mine. I watched as the breath came from his body, but he didn't inhale again. For a moment there was no emotion in me, and then it all hit me all at once. I panicked, and I couldn't think straight. I shook my head and leaned down, slamming my fist against his chest. Tears flooded my eyes and I wept, unable to even get any words out. I was so enveloped by my own grief that I didn't feel the magic began to tingle, or grow, or move up my arm and through my body. Leaning my forehead against Hobbles' shoulder, my eyes clutched tightly, I pressed my palms to him and whispered. "Please, human or not, you're our family and we need you."

As my tears slowed, I began to feel the pulsating of my magic, and I realized, I could no longer hear the voices or the shouting that had been going on around me. I couldn't smell the stench of death or the smoke floating in the air. Slowly I lifted my head and opened my eyes, finding myself encapsulated in an orb of white magic light, just me and Hobbles. I looked down at my hand still firmly pressed against his chest and my eyes went wide as ringlets of energy pulsed down me and into him. The magic had taken hold and my barriers had never gone back up.

I didn't move. I didn't want to. I knew whatever the magic was doing, it was important. For a while, it felt like just my magic, but then I began to feel something else, something familiar. I began to feel Hobbles' magic. It was mixing with mine or the bracelet's, intertwining, moving through him. Then, suddenly, his chest began to move again, and he opened his mouth, taking in a deep breath. His eyes opened wide and shifted straight to me. The magic coming from the bracelet dissipated, and the glow around us receded until we found ourselves right back where we were. Only now, all of the witches were gathered around us and Willa and Shade watched in disbelief as Hobbles reached out his hand for someone to help him to his feet.

I didn't know how I did it, and I wasn't sure

that I'd ever be able to do it again, but the magic in the bracelet had healed Hobbles. Not only was I overjoyed that I had not lost him, but I felt like it was a sign. Despite the impending defeat before Willa and I arrived at the battle, there was hope. Magic hadn't given up, and none of those who possessed it should either.

14

Callie

I DIDN'T LIKE the attention I was getting for what happened with Hobbles.

It wasn't me—it was the bracelet, but nobody really understood that.

Willa kind of understood it, but she still said part of it was me and that it wouldn't have worked for anyone else. I didn't agree with that either. The bracelet didn't come to me, she gave it to me. I still felt like it was a case of mistaken identity. And now, the way people looked at me, thanked me, stared at me in awe was how I imagined that piece of toast felt when the owner said that Jesus' face was toasted onto it. It was all over the news. The miracle piece of toast.

I was the new miracle piece of toast.

At least right then, as the sun set, the attention had left me and was focused on the ceremony at hand. The next two days after the battle was nothing but collecting their dead, preparing them for ceremony, and mourning. I tried to stay out of the way, not wanting to take anything away from those that fought so hard and lost their lives. What surprised me was that the witches even prepared the dark magic witches and beings whose bodies had been left behind. It was an understanding of humanity that actual humans never had.

I stood at the back of the crowd, watching as Shade presented, Hobbles helped, and the witches paid their last respects to their fallen brothers and sisters. The sky was a magnificent rainbow of colors just like Hobbles had described from the Great War. It was interesting though. They weren't buried or cremated. There was no Viking funeral or remains to even clean up. When the ceremony was finished, all of the witches put their arms out and sent their own magic together to blanket the dead. The bodies disappeared, the energy flowing up and outward.

"The magic is never ours," Shade had told me. "Once we're gone, it lives on. It goes back into the cycle. It returns to where it's supposed to be. We have no claim over it."

It all made sense now. And though I was still adamant about Shade flying on a broomstick, I now knew that everything that humans said about witches was crap. It was made up in fantasy. It was almost comical how what I thought was fantasy was actually real and what was real to humans was actually fantasy. I didn't even feel like my human counterparts anymore. And I meant that on multiple levels.

After the battle, the magic didn't all go back into the bracelet like it had before. I could feel it pulsing and humming through my body all the time. I could concentrate on it and bring it to my fingertips, which was more than I could ever do before. As exciting as I thought it would be learning to work with the bracelet's magic, I was actually kind of fearful. I had watched magic destroy lives and I had watched magic bring life back, and those were two really big things to put on my shoulders. My brain really didn't want to accept it, and so I feared it.

I feared that what was doing good, could accidentally do harm. What if I hurt Willa or Shade or Hobbles? What if I defeated the wrong person? It wasn't about who I would answer to or what would happen, it was about not being able to live with myself if that did occur.

Thought after thought ran through my mind during the ceremony, but when it was done, Shade called me, Willa, and Hobbles to the gardens.

"The ceremony is over, and our people will have three days of mourning. There will be no battles, no parties, no celebrations, and most of the city will be shut down. Tonight, the streets will be empty. I've gathered some things and I'd like to go over to my great aunt's house tonight, stake it out from a distance to make sure no one's going in or out, and then if it's clear, go inside and see if we can figure anything out."

All three of us nodded, but none of us were excited about it. Before, it seemed like a new piece of the puzzle. It seemed like we were getting answers, and that was exciting. But there had been a lot of hard growth over the last few days, and we knew that everything we did could lead to the death of others or ourselves. But we also knew one other thing...

"I thought war was heading our way," Shade continued. "But it seems it's already upon us. Without our kings, we are weak. And if we are weak, they will defeat us. If they defeat us, they have control over multiple portals to other realms."

Willa shook her head. "Including the Fae realm."

Hobbles nodded, looking a bit older than he had when he first arrived. "I'm in."

Willa gave a silent nod and so did I. I waited for them to try to convince me to stay behind, but this time they didn't. No one brought it up, and no one even questioned it. In a way, it made me feel good, like they were finally starting to see me as one of them. I had felt like an outsider the whole time. I felt like a burden, someone they had to take care of. I still wasn't ready to go barging in full force, magic at my hands, but I was starting to figure it out slowly.

"Good," Shade said, pushing back his chair and standing up. "They brought some clothes to your rooms, and the best thing to do will be to drive as close as we can get and then walk in. I fear if we use portal magic to get there, we'll alert them. Some witches can sense that. I'll meet you out front in twenty minutes."

I considered making a joke about flying in on broomsticks, but I could tell that Shade was in no mood for jokes, and neither was I really. We all headed silently back to our rooms where there were clothes laid out on our beds. I dressed all in black, pulled my hair back in a ponytail and stared at myself in the mirror for a couple of seconds. I hadn't realized it before, but I looked battle worn and tired. Yet, through all of that, I could still see a glimmer in my eyes, a glimmer that I never had before the bracelet came, or even up to the battle. I wondered if the magic was changing me.

If it was, should I be fearful?

It wasn't time for those kinds of questions. We had a mission, and hopefully we found something at his aunt's house to get us closer to finding the Collector. The stakes were higher, much higher, and it was no longer just finding the Kings, but now it was saving everyone. Just when I thought things couldn't get any crazier, they always did. I was starting to get used to it though.

There was a gentle knock on the door and then it opened before I could say anything. Willa stuck her head in. "You ready?"

I nodded and grabbed my jacket before following her out of the room. In the hallway, I glanced down at her outfit, which was pretty much identical to mine. "So, this is what it takes to get you in a pair of leggings."

She ran her hands down the sides of her thighs. "I guess so. But I have to admit, I kind of like them. I could definitely get used to them. Only, I'd have to have like pink ones or something. I don't think black is good for me."

"I agree," I said with a chuckle. "It makes you look even paler than you already are."

Willa smiled for the first time since before the battle and we headed out to meet everybody at the SUV. I felt like a secret agent, gearing up to go on a mission, only we didn't have any gear. We carried our gear with us in the form of magic. We didn't need any special gadgets or guns. Before heading out, Shade looked in the rearview mirror at us and then over at Hobbles. He didn't say a word, and instead just nodded before taking off.

15

Callie

THE DRIVE to the Freedom Fighters neighborhood, or compound, or whatever it was called, didn't take that long but we parked right outside of it.

It was strange.

As we walked up, I could see the magic that was shielding it from the public. I had never been able to see that before. I stood back and waited as Hobbles and Shade did spells like they did before we entered the witch city, and then nodded to us to follow. We didn't hesitate this time and we knew what to expect. Willa went first and I hopped through afterward, just as amazed by what was on the other side as I was when I went to the witch city.

It was like a little town with dirt roads, small cottages, gardens and flowers everywhere. In the center of the little town was a big house. It wasn't a big house like humans had though. It wasn't draped in lavish marble or perfectly manicured lawns. It just looked like a larger version of the small ones along the way.

We crept through the shadows, and Hobbles did his best to send his magic out in front of us to detect any other essence of dark magic within the town. He was getting a faint reading, but it was too faint for anything to be close by. At the same time though, it was constant. We moved around the right side of the large house, staying on the perimeter at the fence where there were bushes blocking us from view of anybody that may be inside. Everything looked dark and quiet. The four of us settled into our temporary bush home and waited, staking the place out. We wanted to see if anyone was coming and going, or if there was any sign of magic.

The air was warm, the stars were sparkling above, and flickering lights lit up the path throughout the town. If it hadn't been for the fact that we were hunting dark witches, it would've been relaxing. After about two hours sitting there, Shade shook his head and looked over at us. "If they're in there, they're not moving a muscle. This long sitting in the dark, not talking, not moving. I don't think anyone's here."

Hobbles pursed his lips, pulling back the energy he had just sent out. "I'm still getting that constant trace of dark energy, but nothing's changed. There was no spike, and it's not strong enough to be someone literally standing in that house."

"I think we should just go inside and see for ourselves," Willa replied. "Otherwise, we could be sitting here for days. Your brother, my father... The other magical beings, they might not have a few days."

Shade looked back at the house and was quiet for several moments before speaking. "I agree. I think that whatever they came here for they came and left, but hopefully something in there will give me a clue."

We carefully maneuvered ourselves out of the bushes, trying to keep Hobbles quiet as he rolled out with his big stature. We still kept to the shadows just in case, and went around the back, finding the back door unlocked. Shade shook his head at our concerned glances. "When my aunt died, this house became part of the town. She has so many amazing artifacts and beautiful things here that it's kind of a living museum of sorts. Anyone's free to come here and spend time, read, and just be in the space that she was. She was one of the original fighters, and one of only a few who had the stones to keep her alive for so long."

Shade quietly opened the back door and stepped inside, looking around in the dark. Hobbles sent out multiple bursts of energy but when it came back to him, nothing had changed. We crept through all the rooms of the downstairs until we were sure they were clear, and then Shade pulled the curtains and lit the candles in the house. "I don't want to turn on the lights. It will alert somebody that we're here. If there are any enemies, we don't want them to know. But if they're just a town member, we don't want them to come here if there's any kind of danger."

"Good thinking," Hobbles said, patting Shade on the back. "Any idea what we're looking for?"

Shade took in a deep breath and shook his head. "No. I guess anything that'll help us figure out why we were given this address and what the Collector could possibly want from her house. Nothing looks to be out of order. I would say anything that's a magical trinket, any empty spaces that it looks like something was but was taken, and I know that she kept journals. She wrote in them every day until she died. I'm going to go find those. If we can't find anything here, maybe reading through her journals will help me pick up on what they could have possibly wanted from here."

We all split up in different directions with Shade going upstairs and the rest of us taking a section of the lower floor of the house. I carefully poked around the living room, shocked at how much stuff was in there. She had shelves upon shelves against the walls of vials, and stones, and carvings. Everything was incredibly beautiful, but it didn't look like anything that the Collector would want. Of course, I had no idea about the historical relevance of any of it. I was going off of what my bracelet reacted to and what might look suspicious. There were no empty spaces in the living room, and everything was neat and tidy, including being dusted. It seemed that the town took incredibly good care of her house. That was good for the town but made it hard on me to try to find any clues as to what was going on.

The rest of the night was spent there, going through everything, looking for clues, sending out magical vibes, but none of us could find anything out of the normal. I got no reaction from my bracelet to anything in the house except for when I got close to Hobbles or Willa. That was just the bracelet feeding off of them, but it didn't help me at all unless Hobbles had somehow magically been Shade's aunt's cat at some point. I was fairly sure he would've brought up that fact by that point.

Outside, when the sun began to rise, and the first morning dew covered the grass, Shade came downstairs carrying two large boxes. Hobbles immediately went over and took one from him. He set the other one down on the dining room table and looked at us. "Anything?"

I shook my head and so did Willa. Hobbles let out a sigh. "No. Though she did have some weird kitchen utensils in there."

Shade looked at the time. "Well, to avoid any questions by the town, we should go ahead and head out of here. I'm going to take these journals back to the house and start going through them. I wish we had another avenue, but this seems to be the only one at this point. I have no clue why they wanted something from here, or why that address was given to you. It was obviously not a trap, but it also wasn't a clue either. We'll just have to keep digging."

I covered my mouth as I yawned and nodded at Shade in understanding. We loaded up the journals and then jumped back in the SUV and headed back out of town. I pressed my head against the window, feeling the coolness of the glass as we drove, and before I knew it, I had fallen asleep. It wasn't until we got there that Willa tapped me on the shoulder. "Wake up sleepy head. We're back."

Sitting up, I wiped the drool from my chin and realized that I had slept without dreaming for the first time in a long time. It was amazing what exhaustion could do to you. I was dragging my body up the front steps to the house when Shade turned around with his box, almost knocking me backward. He balanced the box on his knee and reached out, grabbing my wrist. "Sorry. You and Willa should get some rest. You guys haven't slept in a while and all I'm gonna be doing is reading these things. You guys can come help whenever you feel like you want to but oth- erwise take this time to rest and recuperate. We may be in a time of mourning right now, but I don't trust the Collector at all. I have no reason to believe he'll show that kind of respect to us."

He turned and went into the house before we could even answer him, but that was fine, he was right. I needed some sleep and some quiet. Who knew how many days we had in front of us before that quiet was gone again? It could be a matter of hours or a matter of weeks, none of us knew.

"I'm going to grab some breakfast and then probably take a snooze myself," Hobbles replied. "You know where to find me."

At that point we all just sluggishly acknowledged each other and headed off in our respectful directions. Shade went toward the library while Willa and I headed back to our rooms. She walked me into my room, sitting down on my bed as I changed my clothes. "How are you feeling about all this?"

I glanced up at her as I took off my socks. "Which part is all of this? Do you mean suddenly having crazy magical powers? Or do you mean everyone looking at me like I'm a miracle worker? Or are we talking about being immersed in a world that I never knew existed?"

Willa laughed. "I guess all of it. Are you holding up okay?"

I shrugged, pulling a sweatshirt on over my head and pushing the hood back. "I'm hanging in there. Not to lie, it's kind of confusing, but what choice do I have? The bracelet is there and it's not going away. The magic is actually starting to work with me, and you're my family so where else would I be? Besides, I think at this point it's gone beyond just supporting you and your father. I'm invested in Shade's people and your people, and all the other beings out there... Well, maybe except for that guy with green teeth. I didn't like him."

"Yeah, he wasn't my first choice either," Willa replied.

I walked over and sat down next to her on the bed. "And how are you doing?"

Willa shrugged, diverting her eyes from mine so I couldn't read them. "I'm okay. I'm definitely better than I was. I think the shop owner was kind of the straw that broke the camel's back. It made me confront everything that was happening instead of just going full speed and trying to fix it. But that's a good thing. I needed to do that. I needed to have that emotion."

I reached over and squeezed her hand and smiled. She took a deep breath, patting me on the leg and stood up. "Get some sleep. If you're not awake by dinnertime, I'm coming to get you so we can eat."

"Perfect," I replied as she walked to the door. "You know how I get when I'm hungry."

As she left the room, Willa made an angry face and clawed the air, hissing. I laughed and waved as she left. I sat there unmoved for a couple more minutes and then reached back, pulling the blankets down. I knew I had a lot to process, but my mind was just too tired. I didn't even know the last time I had gotten sleep besides the catnap in the car. I knew that if I slept, rejuvenated my body, and ate something later that I would feel better and I'd be able think about everything that happened. Until then though, I wasn't going to be any use to anyone.

It didn't take me long to drift off to sleep, but as I did, I thought of Shade. I always thought of Shade, and I was really glad that we went back. No matter what push and pull he gave me, there was still a connection between us that I couldn't deny. Maybe one day he wouldn't deny it either. Then again, I never did have much luck with guys, even hot emo ones.

16

Callie

THE WITCH WORLD had gone eerily quiet.

I understood why, but at the same time, I wasn't used to it. In the human world, funerals were different. Funerals were loud and full of people talking and crying, or singing and praying. But the community was silent. It didn't help that Shade was silent as well. It had been two days at that point since we found his aunt's journals and I had only seen him in passing twice. He didn't come to meals, he didn't come to meetings, and he rarely even went outside.

When I asked if he was sleeping, knowing that Hobbles had checked in on him and helped him with the journals, he just shook his head. "He put some kind of magic spell on himself so he doesn't have to sleep."

"Well, I could've used that in college."

Willa smiled across the dinner table at me. I glanced over at the empty spot where Shade usually sat, his plate untouched, food still spread out across the table. I took a couple more bites of mine and got up, filling his plate full of food, filling his cup with water, and glancing over at the two of them. "Spells or not, he's got to eat something. Besides, I haven't helped him yet with the journals and I'm not going to bed anytime soon. Like all I've been doing is sleeping and wandering around. Let me know if you guys need me for anything."

I ignored that both of them were giving me a sly smile and made my way out of the dining hall and toward the library where Shade was posted up. The door was cracked when I got there so I used my foot to pry it open and carefully made my way through. In the center of the library was a table with what looked like hundreds of journals spread across it. They were stacked up so high that I didn't even see Shade sitting on the other side of the table.

I walked right past him and would've completely missed him if he hadn't cleared his throat. But he didn't do it on my accord. He didn't see me either. "There you are, hiding out in the stack of books. You sound like me when I was thirteen, angsty, and really awkward."

He chuckled but I could tell it was forced. He closed the Journal he was reading and set it on the only neat pile he had, which was what I was assuming was the journals he had already been through.

"I brought you some food. I figured you could use something."

He pushed the journals out of the way as I set the plate in front of him and then handed him a rolled-up set of silverware and his cup of water. Shade leaned back in the chair and rolled his shoulders as he leaned his head back. "I appreciate it. I was starting to get hungry. Everything okay out in the castle?"

I shrugged. "You mean besides Hobbles walking around in your tapestries and Willa swinging from the chandeliers and painting everything a bright pink? It's totally fine."

He laughed again but this time it was not so

forced. I sat down next to him as he ate, looking around at the stacks and piles. "Did she write every moment of her life down in these?"

He swallowed his bite of food. "Basically. But from what Hobbles tells me, she didn't actually write these, she transferred her memories to these. So, it's basically her account from inside of her mind. Right now, I'm just getting to the part where she's upset about the way the witches are being treated. She hasn't even joined the Freedom Fighters yet."

I puffed out my cheeks, not quite knowing what to say. "Well, I'm here to help. Just put me where you want me to start, and I will get to it."

He nodded at the pile. "I don't even care about going in order anymore. The dates are at the top of each one. Just grab one and start reading. If there's anything you think might be something that would lead the Collector to my aunt's house, just let me know and I'll look it over."

I grabbed a journal and set it down in front of me, opening it up to the first page. "So, you didn't spend a lot of time with her?"

"Just about the same amount of time that any-body spends with the third-generation aunt who is kind of strange and you are not really sure what to talk with them about. My father used to visit her a lot. As kids I can remember going over there and she always had candy and cakes, and she always had so many cool things to look at. Most of the conversations that were had were between her and my father. When I was older, I was busy taking care of my brother all the time, and he had duties all the time, so I barely saw anyone. I did go to her funeral, which was just as eclectic as she was, and had to be held outside of the city because basically the entire witch community came to it."

"Wow. She really was important to this community," I said. "I'm pretty sure if I died, it would be Willa, and now you, Hobbles, and maybe the other Fae, but it really depends."

Shade shoveled another bite into his mouth. "Everybody always puts so much emphasis on that when they're alive, but in the end, who cares? I won't know. A million people could show up, or one person could show up, and I would never know the difference. But I could see how it helps to comfort those who are mourning the loss of somebody. To know they were that important to the community. I was definitely proud that she was my aunt. I just didn't know her personally very well."

As Shade ate, obviously hungrier than what he

had led on to be, I started to read through the Journal I picked out. It read like a narrative, and it was very descriptive. However, with small gaps here and there I could see what he meant by she'd transferred her memories to paper. Obviously, he meant that magically, and just like any other being, there were gaps in her memory. But there was one thing that stood out to me almost immediately. I flipped back and looked at the date, realizing it was a good six years after the journal that he was reading had been written.

"Huh," I said, sitting up and pushing the journal toward Shade. "Did you know that your aunt helped to protect more than just the town, but magical beings from all realms? They were brought to her, or she would find them and then she would move them through what she describes as a series of tunnels. It says that a lot of them lived in those tunnels until it was safe to come out."

Shade nodded nonchalantly. "Yeah, that's one of the big reasons why everyone loved her so much. The dark magic witches on the governing boards tried to take her down multiple times but they could never find these... Wait..." He rolled his eyes and fell back in his chair, slapping his palm to his forehead. "How could I have been so stupid? How could I have not even thought of this? The tunnels that she's talking about, I've been in there before. I was like nine years old with my brother, and our father wanted us to see a big part of our history and teach us about it. So, he took us to the tunnels. But they're not so much tunnels as they are caves."

"Where do they go?"

"All over. But most of them went to places where portals could be opened up so that magical beings stuck here could get back to their realms unscathed by the battling going on in the Great War. A lot of them were also used to move witches to other realms to keep them safe until the war was over. Apparently, shortly after she joined the fighters, or founded the fighters, she began working on these tunnels a little at a time. She used her magic to core out these walkways underground. The outside of it is limestone and bedrock. There's something about the limestone that keeps other magical beings from really sensing what's going on."

I thought about it for a second and shook my head. "Are these tunnels underneath the house?"

Shade nodded his head. "They are."

"So, when we were there, the dark magic that Hobbles was feeling, that could've been coming from there right?" I felt like we just had a breakthrough.

Shade nodded his head emphatically. "Absolutely. Which means they may have been right under our feet the whole time. Which means if we go back there right now, we might actually be able to find my brother, Willa's father, and the Collector."

I pushed the seat back from the table and jumped up. The magic was running through me and so was the adrenaline. "I gotta go tell Willa and find Hobbles."

Shade reached up and grabbed my arm. It caught me off guard, just having him touch me. I hated that he had that effect on me. "Hold on. Hobbles is too big. Just his height alone would make it really difficult for him to fight in an enclosed space. And Willa, well she doesn't have a lot of magic right now and we could get her killed. I understand the emotion that goes behind realizing that you might be able to save your family, but for Willa, it could get her killed."

I shook my head. "What does that mean? Are we leaving without them? They might kill us."

Shade stood up and smiled at me. "Think about it this way. If we don't come back, we're already dead. If we do come back, we either have both of the Kings, or at least a way better idea of how to get them. We can handle their anger then."

It was a terrible idea. It was a terrible idea that I was actually going to go along with. I didn't know if he was playing for my emotions or not, but the thought of anything happening to Willa or Hobbles was too hard to think about. Then again, why would he play me in that situation?

Shade tossed the journal he was reading in the pile and started to walk out of the library. "Come on. I'll meet you in the garden in ten minutes. We've got this."

Did we? Because Shade's sudden nonchalant attitude about danger was more than a little bit curious. But what choice did I have? I hadn't distrusted Shade before, and I was going to do my best not to start now.

17

Willa

I NEVER MEANT to sleep that long, but after stuffing my face at dinner with Hobbles, and Callie off talking to Shade, I had nothing else to do.

I laid down for an after-dinner nap. I curled up in a ball, sank myself into the covers and just let things go. A year ago, if you had told me that I would feel comfortable sleeping at the witch compound, I would've told you that you were crazy. But after everything going on, I probably felt more comfortable there than at home, at that point. At least there I knew I had help protecting Callie, and in all honesty, protecting me.

Not being able to do much magic never bothered me while I was living in the human world. In fact, it was one of the major sticking points when I decided to leave the Fae realm and start a life here. But ever since the danger started, and after I took a trip to the Fae realm, I was feeling exceptionally helpless. I wanted to be able to protect myself, protect others, and find my father. But it would make sense why the Collector would bring him here. He would know that I wouldn't be able to protect myself really. I definitely wouldn't be able to fight him for my father. I hated feeling helpless.

I stretched my arms over my head, groaned and looked over at the time. I hadn't slept as long as I thought. It was only about 10 o'clock. It just seemed later because everybody was so silent. It was still a time of mourning. I took my time getting dressed, figuring I would go hang out with Callie for a little while, or help with the journals. I had nothing else to do and I was starting to get bored. I thought about going back home and checking on everything, but I knew that idea wouldn't go over well with everyone else. The Collector wanted me, he wanted Callie, and he wanted anybody else that was involved.

I quietly closed my door and stopped by Callie's room just in case she had already come back, but I peeked in and she wasn't there. I headed over to the library, but all I found was a stack of journals, but neither of them were there. It wouldn't have been weird if it was only Shade there, but with Shade gone too and Callie not in her room, a warning signal was going off in my head. I flipped off the lights in the library and closed the door behind me. As soon as I turned, a loud booming explosion erupted outside. It shook everything so hard that I had to hold on to the walls to keep my footing. My stomach leapt into my chest, and as soon as I got my feet back on the ground, I took off down the hallway toward the main corridor.

As I rounded the corner, I ran straight into Hobbles. He grabbed me by the shoulders to keep me from falling down. "The dark witches are back, and they're more prepared this time. Did Shade feel the explosion?"

I blinked at him several times. "I thought you would've already talked to him. He's not in the library."

The look on Hobbles' face was one of concern. "He wasn't in his room or outside. Most everybody I asked said that they hadn't seen him in days."

I didn't understand. "How can two people just disappear?"

"Two?"

I led Hobbles back to the library. "Yeah, I came here to talk to Callie. But she's not in her room and she said she would be here, but she's not here either. Do you think they're in the garden?"

Hobbles walked around the table and looked down at the journal that was spread open. He scanned the page and stood there, quietly sorting through whatever he had running in his mind. I was trying not to be impatient, but my nerves were through the roof. "Hobbles?"

He shook himself back. "Sorry, no, they aren't in the garden. I walked past there on my way inside. But this journal talks about his aunt when she started the safe passageway for all magical beings. She calls it a tunnel... But I've been in it and it's not a tunnel."

He immediately hurried around the table and toward the door. I ran after him, not having any idea what he was talking about. "Hobbles! Wait! Tell me what you're talking about."

He didn't respond to me. I caught up to him and grabbed him by the arm. "Hey!"

He was breathing heavily, his eyes shifting back and forth. "I saw the tunnel when it was first finished. His aunt created it with magic, but it took her almost six years. It's more like a cave, narrow spaces, and underground, hidden under the limestone."

A lightbulb went off in my head. "And it's hard for other magical beings to sense magic, especially light magic under limestone for some reason."

"But dark magic... A lot easier to detect because it's more potent. And I was detecting it. The entire time we were at his aunt's house."

My mouth dropped open. "Oh my God! The tunnels are under the house and they went there to find the Kings. Why would they not take us with them?"

"Well, it's a really small space and for a guy my size, it makes it really hard to fight. As far as you... I'm assuming because you don't have your full powers and Callie is terrified now that one of us will die. I don't know why Shade would go along with it, but then again, he showed that he cares for all of us. He also hasn't slept in days."

I pointed toward the door. "We have to get

there. Now. And we have to tell Shade about what's happening here. We're under attack, and we need his leadership."

I couldn't believe Callie would make such a bad decision, but then again, I would've done the same thing for her. I just hoped that by the time I got to yell at her, she was still alive. I hoped that they were both alive. Otherwise, we were all doomed.

1 8

Callie

"Watch your head," Shade said, going down the stairs in front of me.

We came directly back to the house and Shade had remembered that the entrance was somewhere in the basement.

"I really hate basements," I groaned as I swatted away a cobweb. "They're always creepy and dark."

Shade put out his hand and helped me down the last few steps. "I always liked basements," he replied. "They're quiet, empty, and usually nobody bothers you."

I rolled my eyes as I wiped my hands on the sides of my pants, snarling at the spiders in the rafters above. "Yeah, but you're a witch. An emo witch that lives in a dark castle. I feel like if anybody's going to love basements, it's going to be you."

Shade chuckled, leading me between the rows of boxes and cleaning materials toward a bookcase at the back. "Did you just call me creepy and dark like a basement?"

Before I could answer, I spotted a broom. "Look, you guys just park your cars anywhere."

Shade gave me his normal roll of the eye and then walked up to the bookshelf, putting his hands on his hips and staring at the dusty shelves. There were tons of books on there, but none of them had any titles on the binding. Well, none of them except for one. When Shade found it, he grinned, reaching up and pulling it forward. As he did, the spell disappeared from over it and it revealed itself as a handle. It clicked and behind us, a latch flew open in the floor.

He walked up next to me and grinned. "It might've been a long time, but I remembered. You ready?"

My bracelet had already picked up in intensity, and I knew it probably had something to do with the dark magic that Hobbles had been sensing the last time we came there. There I was, without Willa or Hobbles. It was strange, I had hoped to be alone with Shade for a very long time, but now that I was in the situation that I was in, I really wished my friends were there. I was in a no-win situation. I had no other choice but to move forward.

Shade went first, taking a step down through the hatch and looking back at me. I took a deep breath, finding my boldness or what was left of it and followed him down. It was dark at first, and I had a hard time finding my footing. I reached out and put my hand on his shoulder, making sure that I didn't take a tumble all the way to the bottom. Slowly, we made our way down the winding, rough, staircase. It was far beneath the earth, much further than I anticipated. The lower we went, the colder it got. We were descending down that staircase for nearly five minutes before a faint light began to illuminate the stairwell.

Shade's demeanor almost instantly changed. The excitement and playfulness of before slipped away, and his face grew serious. We slowed our pace, moving closer to the wall as we approached the doorway. I could smell a faint hint of sulfur in the air. I hated that smell. It was like rotten eggs and wet dog.

At the bottom of the steps, Shade paused, putting his hand behind him, touching my leg. Had I not been horribly terrified at what we were walking into, I might have noticed, but my body was poised for battle, not for flirting. Carefully, he peaked around the corner and then began to move again. We followed the hallway for what seemed like ages, pausing as other doorways appeared, splitting the tunnel off in different directions. However, those areas were unlit, so we thought it best to follow the torches hovering against the cave walls instead.

Twisting and turning, we moved through the hallways, listening for any sounds or presence. My bracelet was humming like crazy, and I could barely hear my own thoughts by the time we turned the twentieth turn in the corridor. As we did, Shade reached over and pressed me back against the wall, putting his finger to his lips. My heart dropped and I closed my eyes for a moment, listening through my magic, to the sound of faint voices ahead. I couldn't make out what they were saying, but one was deep and familiar.

As soon as I heard the voice, I knew it was the

Collector. I opened my eyes wide, looking down the hallway. The lights flickered, casting eerie shadows across the cave walls and I could feel the moisture against my back. Down at the end, a familiar sight came into view. It was an archway, the same archway that had been in my dream over and over again. I pressed my hand against Shade and pushed him back, slowly walking forward. Everything that I had seen, and everything I had dreamt for the last few weeks was laid out in front of me. It was right then that I realized something. My dreams weren't dreams after all. They were premonitions.

I knew what awaited me through the archway, but I also knew there was no other way. Without any thought at all, I took off, running straight for the archway. I could hear Shade behind me, calling out for me, but I ignored him, knowing what my destiny was. I didn't slow as I reached the doorway. I knew that if I did, I would stop and not go through. So instead, I took a deep breath, mustering every bit of bravery that I had left in me and threw myself through the doorway.

As I stumbled out, I found myself exactly where I thought I would be, in the open expanse of gray. I came to a stop and looked all around me, seeing the white lingering souls that floated just above the surface like fog and mist. I turned to look back and the doorway was gone, opening up to what seemed like a never-ending world of nothingness. There was an emptiness to it, something that breached even my outer shell and sunk into me like it was clasping on to the layers upon layers of my heart.

"The Collector waits for you," a voice said from behind me.

I paused, not immediately turning around, knowing I had reached the part of my visions I was never able to go past. That voice though, was not in anything I had dropped in the days leading up to that moment. Very slowly I began to turn around, my eyes landing on a beautiful woman, her body bluish in color, her hair flowing all around her as if she were weightless. Her features were demure and fragile, but I could see the strength in her movements. Her face was calm, no fear or emotion in her eyes.

I knew almost immediately who she was. "I see you left the house."

"I've been waiting for you," she replied. "I could not stay long in one place, as the Collector has control over my world."

I glanced around. "Is this your world?"

She nodded. "Part of it."

I shook my head. "Where are we?"

Without warning, her body raced forward, her feet, not even touching the ground. She stopped just inches away and placed her hands on mine. "We do not have time. I can only keep you here for a moment. You must defeat the Collector as he comes for all realms, not just your own. The bracelet is the key, but many will die before the resolution. You cannot do it alone, but you must find the people who can help you. I will do my best to protect the kings until you can retrieve them, but hope lies within the powers you possess."

I shook my head. "I don't possess powers. I'm a human. The only powers I have are in that bracelet."

A small smile moved across her lips, and it was the only type of emotion that she showed. "Magic only works on those who naturally would be able to possess it in the first place. You may have been given the bracelet, but the bracelet facilitated that. It was meant for you." Suddenly her eyes shifted up and her hands gripped tighter against me. "You must go. The bracelet can only shield you for so long from the eye of the Collector. Protect your friends, and I will see you again."

Before I could ask another question, I found myself spiraling through a space much like a portal. However, it was far more short-lived of a trip than any portal that I had been in. I came flying out of it, landing on the cold cave floor in the center of the room, through the archway. There was loud shouting and flashes of magic all around me. I looked up to find Shade, battling the dark robed figures. He was far outnumbered. Without thought, I jumped to my feet and raced over next to him. He blasted a wall of magic outward, hitting the first row of dark beings.

"Where did you go?" he asked, still throwing magic in the other direction. "I came to the door and you weren't here. But there are plenty of the Collector's little minions."

I shook my head. "To another realm of some sort. The banshee was there. I…" Suddenly, Shade threw his arm up in front of me, creating a shield against the magic that was flying toward me. We both stumbled backward against the wall of the cave. The dark entities raced toward us. We were trapped and cornered. The magic came from the bracelet quick and without thought, and my hands immediately went up. Before I could let off a shot though, a loud booming voice stopped the dark entities in their tracks.

"Do not harm her! She is mine! Something pretty for my collection!"

My jaw clenched and my eyes narrowed, watching as the dark entities stopped and moved to the side, creating an open path in front of me. At the end of that path, the Collector stepped from the shadows, draped in black robes, his eyes and face hidden within the dark shadows of his hood, and the only semblance of a person that could be seen were his white, frail hands dangling from the sleeves of his robe. A frosty wind whipped through the cave, wrapping itself around me. I groaned and gripped my chest, falling to my knees. I knew that feeling. How could I ever forget it? The Collector had been the one in the portal to reach through and grab me. It was his icy hand that held me in the portal, just as it was holding me with its magic in that moment.

"I knew you would come," the Collector said, slowly drifting forward. "I didn't think the plan would work. I thought it was too simple, but even through all of your magic, you cannot break away from the ignorance of your human being."

"It was a trap," Shade hissed. "The whole thing was a set up."

"Yes," the Collector hissed. "All the way down to the shop owner that the poor little Fae had watched die. See what empathy gets you? The Princess didn't even see my men slip him the piece of paper because she was so worried about his life. I was hoping that she would be here. Three of you would really brighten up my collection. But no matter, I'll have time to find her later. For now, there are many things that I need to do with you."

"Keep your hands off of her!" Shade struggled, but it seemed he was being controlled by something, bound with his hands back.

"Stupid witch," the Collector roared. "Just like your brother, too worried about other people's safety to save yourself. But no matter, I can sense I don't need you anyway. Whatever magic you have in you is already in the bracelet, and with it, Callie herself. Disposing of you would bring me great pleasure, but I think even more so if I watched your brother do it for me."

The Collector snapped his fingers and to the right, Shade's brother appeared, held on each side by a dark entity, his eyes weak and saddened. To the left, another man appeared in the same condition, and when his eyes lifted to mine, I knew exactly who he was. I could see Willa in his face. He was a King, but the spark that lit the Fae world was quickly fading from his eyes. I gripped my hand into a fist, slowly lowering it and readying myself. But before I could attempt any kind of magic, the Collector threw his arm up, and magic, a dark magic that I could feel sifting through me, just like before, gripped me by the neck and lifted me from my feet.

The Collector clicked his tongue and shook his head. "No, no. Let the witches play. Besides, we have plenty of time for your magic. First, though, I want you to watch your friend die."

19

Callie

"Stand up," the Collector yelled toward Shade's brother.

The Collector used his magic to control the Witch King, forcing him to his feet. I could see the King fighting the magic, but he was far too weak. The Collector lifted the King's hands, and magic moved through the King, swirling around his fists. Shade's brother shook his head, tears rolling down his eyes. "No, I will not do it."

The Collector laughed. "You will do it. You

will kill him, or I will take your life and the life of every single one of your people."

The Witch King was trembling, and Shade looked up at him, calm and collected. "Brother, it's okay. You're strong, and your duty lies with our people. You can save them."

The Collector bellowed out in laughter. "Do it!"

The Witch King shook his head, with tears running down his cheeks, but Shade nodded at him and closed his eyes. I screamed out, but nobody seemed to notice. I struggled against the binds that held me, and it was to no avail. The Witch King closed his eyes as well and everything moved in slow motion. The orb of witch magic flowed from his hands and sped straight towards Shade. I clenched my eyes closed, knowing I couldn't watch, not another death. A loud crackle sounded out, booming like thunder through the cave.

My heart sank and tears spread down my cheeks. My body stopped struggling and slowly, I opened my eyes. However, Shade was not dead. In front of him was a wall of magic sparking and sizzling as the Witch King's magic slammed into it and dissipated into the cave ground.

"Not today Collector." Hobbles' voice came

from the opening of the cave, and instantly hope filled me again.

The Collector grabbed the Fae King and stepped behind him just as Willa stepped from behind Hobbles. The magic holding me and Shade released us. I fell to the ground, grasping my neck. Willa slowly took a few steps forward, her lips trembling as she stared at her father. "Daddy?"

Before we could react, Willa went rushing forward, running straight for her father. I jumped to my feet and bolted toward her, but not before the Collector could swat her away, sending her flying backward. I dove forward, contacting Willa. I grabbed her around the waist and we fell to the ground.

"Stupid girl," the Collector grumbled. "The witches, the most powerful beings in this realm can't defeat me, but you think you can? The Fae have no power here! Before long, the Fae will have no power whatsoever, and neither will the witches."

Both Willa and I were on our hands and knees, and I glanced over at her as she put her hand on top of mine and gripped onto it. She gave me a knowing nod and a wink. I suddenly realized that everything she was doing was on purpose. I grinned at her and gave her a small nod back, helping her to her feet. As the Collector droned on about his magical powers, holding tightly to the Fae King as protection, Willa and I grasped hands. I glanced back at Hobbles, and Shade who had noticed what we were doing and preparing themselves.

"You know what the problem is with you, Collector?" I asked, as I put my hand behind my back and counted down from three. "You're so caught up in yourself and destroying everything, that you don't even see what's right in front of your nose. You won't win. You will lose, and we will be there to see it."

The Collector began to cackle nefariously as my fingers counted down to one, and then my hand closed into a fist. As it did, Shade and Hobbles threw their magic outward, pushing back as many of the dark entities as they possibly could. The Collector's eyes went wide, and then shifted over to Callie and me just as we gripped down, sending our magic flying out in all directions. It toppled all of the dark entities, and tossed the Collector backward, still gripping onto Willa's father. The magic this time moved smoothly through us, not harshly like the time before.

As the last of it radiated out from us, I lunged

forward to grab Willa's father, but the Collector had already pulled him back into the corner. He growled at the two of us, and swished his arm through the air, pulling the Fae King into the portal with him. They were gone before we could even get halfway to them. Instantly, I turned toward the Witch King who was staring at Shade, ten feet apart. The Witch King smiled, opening his mouth to say something, but before he could, a portal opened behind him, and two arms reached through, grabbing him around the body, yanking him backward.

Shade called out in fear and raced forward, but the portal slammed shut before he could get him. Willa fell to her knees and shook her head, slamming her fists on the ground. Suddenly, all around us, the cave began to shake and quake. Shade looked up and around as he ran toward us. "There's a failsafe in these caves. It was put here when my aunt built them. If it senses an overload of dark magic, they will collapse. The witches thought it better to die within the caves then be captured by the dark magic.

I shook my head, grabbing Willa by the shoulders and lifting her to her feet. "Why didn't it go off till now?"

Hobbles hurried over, pulling us all into a

group. "The Collector must've been holding it back, but now that he's gone, there's nothing to stop it."

Shade gave a nod, returning to his normal serious tone. "Let's get back to the witch Castle."

Willa shook her head. "We can't. Droves of dark witches attacked. By the time we got out of there, they were overrunning everything. From what we can tell, they attacked the witch city too. No one is safe."

The cave rattled again, and boulders fell in front of the archway. Shade put his hand out. "Let's get to safety and we can figure it all out from there."

Without thought, everyone put their hand on Shade's, and we were instantly thrown into the portal. As I entered, though, my body began to shut down, and the exhaustion washed over me. I could still hear the Collector laughing in my head as we raced toward wherever Shade was taking us. Before I could reach the exit though, my eyes lost the fight. Everything went dark. The last thing I remembered was the sound of my body hitting the ground.

SHADE

I stood there, on the field that led up to the witch Castle, watching the remnants of my home simmer in large piles of ash and fire. All around me, bodies were laid strewn on the ground, my brothers and sisters who had fought as hard as they could but were overtaken. Sadness overwhelmed me, and the guilt that followed threatened to break me. I was responsible for these people. I was the one that was supposed to care for them, to protect them in my brother's stead, and I failed at that. But I knew one thing was for sure, I would not fail at finding my brother and bringing him back to safety.

There wasn't much I could do there at that point. The witches that had survived the attacks were spread out, racing off for protection. After getting Callie safely back to her home and leaving her to Hobbles' and Willa's care, I had to come back to the castle to check on everyone. It seemed, though, after helping a few people left over, there was much more I could do. I had to focus on what I could, and that was helping Callie and the others and getting my brother back.

I took one last sad look around and teleported myself to the city, high above on the rooftops, so I could look down without fear of being seen. What I found was just about what I expected. Fires raged all across the city, screams could be heard in the distance, and dark witches marched the city streets, acting as if they had overtaken the city. Of course, I guess that's exactly what it was. I didn't stay there very long, not wanting to be found out. I quickly teleported again, heading back to Callie's house.

I landed in the front yard, and several of the guards that I had sent, and those that had volunteered, nodded over at me. There were witches coming and going from the house, and though there was a protection spell put over the space and a shielding spell so that the neighbors couldn't see what was happening, with as many people that had arrived there, I wasn't sure how long the spell would hold. Hobbles was working on it, though.

No one really knew how it happened, but Callie's house had become sort of a sanctuary to our people. When I had left, Callie still hadn't woken up, so she had no idea. But Willa took them in immediately, showing them the grace and compassion that the Fae were known for. She never even batted an eye, and I was very grateful for her and to her for providing a safe space for everyone.

Walking into the house, things did not look anything like they used to. When so many witches began to show up, we quickly realized that there wouldn't be enough space to house all of them. But instead of sending them somewhere else, we created a magical spell that practically quadrupled the amount of space in Callie's house without anyone around being able to see it. It was a pretty ingenious idea. It was not one of my own, though, it was the idea of one of the elder witches that had been brought there when they left the city.

All across the house, there were voices, blankets, food, and even some laughter. As witches, we weren't the kind of people to take advantage of anyone's hospitality, so when everyone got there, they immediately went to work, making sure that everyone was fed, that Willa was taken care of, and that the atmosphere was safe but also comforting. Callie had a whole team of healers checking on her, yet not a single one of them understood why she was unconscious. One of the Seers even tried to look into her mind and see if she was dreaming, but she said that there was nothing but calmness. I could only assume it was because of the magic and the toll it took on her human body. I hoped that she woke up soon, but I also wanted to be there when she saw her house for the first time. It would definitely be comical.

Rounding the corner into the enlarged kitchen, glancing over the multitude of burners and stoves and cauldrons, I spotted Willa at the back corner, tasting a bite of one of the elder's soups. I made my way through, nodding at everyone as they smiled and waited until Willa was finished.

"That's delicious," she told the elder. "Thank you so much."

She glanced over at me and politely stepped away, walking with me back through the cauldrons and into the pantry area that had been stocked with everything that they could need at the house. "How's everything going?"

Willa took in a deep breath and looked around her. "Amazing. Your people have really made sure that everyone is taken care of. They've got rounds of witches teleporting to different places. They know they can collect food, medicine, and anything else they might need. Elders are constantly cooking, and even the kids have something to do. There hasn't been any sign of trouble so far."

"Good," I replied. "It's important that they not go back to the city, or the house. The main house is gone pretty much, and the city has been overrun by dark witches. Anything from Callie yet?"

Willa hung her head in disappointment. "Nothing. Hobbles is up there with her now, taking a shift, and I'll go back up when it's done. The healers have been burning candles, spells, chants, and anything else they could think of to try to help her snap out of it. But physically, there's nothing wrong with her. From the out-side, it just looks like she's asleep."

I put my hand on Willa's shoulder. "She'll be okay. She's in good hands, and when she's ready, she'll come out of it."

"Oh," Willa said before I could walk away. "There was one thing. One of the healers said that there was an incredible amount of energy coming from her bracelet, the same energy that flows through her. They said that they think that the bracelet is the one bringing the witches here."

I half-smiled. "I feel like the bracelet has taken on Callie's personality. She would've done some-thing like this, just to keep people safe."

Willa smiled. "Yeah, and she would've been

incredibly stressed out by it but would've never wanted it any other way."

We both glanced up at the ceiling, knowing that just over our heads, Callie rested in her bed, soft and serene, no movement coming from her. But I knew that was just a deception. I knew that inside, Callie was doing something, and for some reason, she wasn't ready to come back. But the longer she stayed under, the more danger she was in. If we were attacked, with all the people at that house, I wasn't sure that I could get to Callie in time to save her. Whatever she was doing, she was leaving it up to us to care for people and to protect her until she was ready. I didn't trust a lot of people, but I had learned to trust Callie very quickly. And if she needed protection, then that was what I was going to give her. It was hoped that she came out of it soon.

What are you doing in there, Callie? Come back to us. We need your help. We're here, and we're waiting, but I don't know how long that'll last.

A month before, I would've been much more fearful for Callie than I was then. It wasn't that I didn't think Callie was in trouble, but I had seen her grow and strengthen, especially over the last couple of weeks. Whether the bracelet was controlling her or she was controlling the bracelet, it didn't matter. She was getting stronger by the day, and there would come a time that she was stronger than any of us. There was much more to Callie than met the eye, and I knew in my gut that we had to protect her. Without her, I wasn't sure if any of us would survive.

20

Callie

I OPENED MY EYES, finding myself staring up at a deep cerulean sky.

Violet petals floated across my vision, and I watched as one came straight toward me, landing on my cheek. When I picked up my arm to brush it away, I realized I was wet. In fact, I was floating on the top of a perfectly still body of water, everything besides the sky and the petals a muted gray. I was dressed in a white cotton gown, with lace on the shoulders and the kind of layers that you would see on a dress that a princess wore in some movie.

"Hello, Callie," a familiar soothing voice said, reaching her hand down to help me up.

Standing above me was the banshee, only now, she was no longer blue, her face had expressions, and she smiled at me kindly, waiting patiently for me to take her hand. She was standing on top of the water, and as she lifted me to my feet, I found myself doing the same. I looked around us, finding the atmosphere familiar, but I couldn't place it. "Where are we?"

We walked along the surface of the water and over to the bank into soft, lush grass. The banshee held her hands tightly in front of her and smiled as we walked. "This place? This is where I grew up. I spent many years walking across the pond, dancing around in the falling petals, and dreaming of a life that I was not destined to have."

I looked around the space. The colors were beautiful, the world alive but much different than the human realm. "It's beautiful here. It's much better than the last place we met."

The banshee stopped and turned toward me, snapping her fingers. The beauty and wonder of the place around me disappeared, and we were back on the empty Great Plains where the spirits roamed. "It is actually the same place. Many, many years ago, the darkness began to creep into our realm. It was like a plague, infecting everything it touched. There was nothing we could do."

"I'm sorry," I said, not really sure what else to say. "What is this place?"

"This place is many things. It is where my people are born and raised, and it is also where lost souls are brought to live and wander for eternity. Those souls were kept within certain confines of our land, but when the darkness came, they were released. But that is not why I brought you here."

The souls all along the ground began to whip wildly, swaying back and forth and folding upward into full stature. They surrounded us, making no noise, just standing there. The banshee didn't seem to even notice. She just stared straight at me, watching my face. Slowly her body began to fade into that shade of blue again, and I realized that what had happened to her world also happened to her.

"I brought you here because this is where the Collector has sent the Witch King. He is being kept here by a magical binding that can only be undone by magic just as strong. You have to find him and unbind him, and then he can be released. But it's important to know that he is a living soul among beings that have been turned into nothing but lost souls. Each moment that he is here is a moment that is taken from his life. When those moments run out, he will become part of this realm."

My mouth dropped open just a bit. I had to admit, things were getting weirder and weirder by the second. Each time I thought it couldn't get any stranger, something new happened. "But how am I supposed to find him? I'm not even in my body right now. I'm in my mind."

The banshee turned toward the souls and spread her arms wide. They dispersed, racing off in other directions, moaning and wailing as they went. She turned back to me and placed her hands back in front of her calmly. "The bracelet does many things. Long ago, when the realms were new and the creatures roamed. a stone wrapped in a metal vine landed in each of the realms. It was that stone that gave the magic to all the worlds everywhere. There was one stone per realm. All the leaders got together and met, bringing a piece of metal with them. That metal was forged into that bracelet. The Fae were the keepers of the bracelet and had been since the first of the realms emerged. That bracelet has been guarded by the Fae and holds pieces of magic that has been lost by the realms."

I looked down at the bracelet and lifted my brow. "Well, I'm assuming Willa didn't know that when she put it on my wrist. She should be the one doing all of this."

The banshee smiled kindly and shook her head. "The bracelet chooses who it works through. If Willa gave you the bracelet, then the bracelet willed her to do so. It is you that is strong enough to wield this immense power, but you have to grow with it. The bracelet will help you find the King of the Witches. But you must hurry. Everything fades away in time…"

As the banshee spoke, she began to disappear from in front of me. Her voice was trailing like the wind. "Do not let the Witch King fade away. He plays a very important role in what is to come in the future. I cannot contact you unless I am able to escape the roving eye of the Collector, but I will be with you in thought."

When she had completely disappeared, every-thing went black. I stood there in the silence of nothingness for several moments before I closed my eyes. When I opened them again, I was lying in bed, the covers pulled up to my chest, staring at my very own ceiling. At my feet was my dog, and in my chair next to the bed was Hobbles still in his human form. I blinked my eyes several times and put my hands down, pulling myself up in the bed. Hobbles had fallen asleep in his chair, but my movement woke him.

He jumped up and hurried to my side. "Callie, you're awake. Everyone's been waiting. How are you feeling? I'll go get the healer."

I reached out and grabbed his arm and shook my head. "I'm okay. How long have I been asleep?"

"About three days now," he replied. "Some things have changed…"

I lifted an eyebrow. "That's never a good sign."

Slowly I pulled myself from my bed, feeling quite relaxed and well for someone that had been sleeping for three days. I stretched my arms up over my head and brought them down, rolling my shoulders. When I glanced at my wrist. I noticed that the bracelet was still there, but it had further combined with my body. It looked as if threads of metal had been sown through my skin. It didn't hurt and was actually less intense than before we had come to our house.

"I need to talk to Willa and Shade. Will you show me to them?"

Hobbles immediately stood up and put his arm out for me to take. I smiled and lifted myself to my feet, not knowing what to expect. I felt more energized than ever. But I took his arm just in case. When he opened the door to my room, though, I stumbled a bit, and it had nothing to do with not being awake for three days. Instead of the hallway wall I was used to seeing, my living room had grown seven times in size, and to my left was an enormous kitchen that I couldn't even see the other side of. Slowly, I looked up, hearing voices, and found multiple levels had been added to the house. And the expansion was just the beginning of it.

Everywhere that I turned, there were witches. There were witch families, witch children, older witches stirring cauldrons and cooking things. The entire house was full of witches. Hobbles must've seen my confusion. "After you passed out, witches just came pouring into the house. We believe that the bracelet was calling them here to safety. They used their magic to expand your house and have been taking care of everyone here. It's been interesting. But they all have questions about you, and I'm starting to think they believe you're some sort of omen or prophet."

I chuckled nervously as we walked along, everyone stopping as I passed and either looked at me curiously or smiled and whispered to someone else. I felt like I was back in grade school all over again right after I got that horrible haircut. When we reached the other side of the house, Hobbles opened the back door and showed me out into what had been magically turned into an enormous garden. Way overhead, I could see a dome of protective magic.

Out in the center of the garden Willa, stood, pointing at the different plants as she talked to a few of the witches. Sitting on the bench next to it was Shade with one of his aunt's journals in his hands, carefully studying it. The Journal looked burnt and singed, and my anxiety began to rise.

As soon as Willa saw me though, she let out a shrill shriek and came running toward us, throwing herself into me and hugging me so tightly, I could barely breathe. Shade walked up, and I glanced up at him, silently asking for help. He chuckled and tapped Willa on the back. "You're going to kill her."

Willa released quickly and giggled, a sound

that was more than needed at that moment. "How are you feeling? Well, besides overwhelmed at what you see here."

I chuckled as I looked around. "Yeah, this is all a little bit confusing, but I can ask questions about that later. While I was sleeping, I met someone."

Willa raised a brow. "Okay. But you really think this is a good time to be dating?"

I blinked at her several times before shaking my head and looking over to Shade. "The banshee took me to her realm. Again, only when I first woke there, it was beautiful, but she explained that the darkness had crept in many, many years ago, and basically the lost souls had taken it over."

Shade rubbed his arms as if he were spooked. "The lost realm. That's where you went when you entered in through the archway in the cave, right?"

I nodded at him. "But we didn't just have a nice little chat. Shade, I know where your brother is. He has hidden and bound in that world, and we have to find him before he becomes a lost soul. The banshee told me that the bracelet will show me the way. She also told me hell was formed. That's an interesting story. Regardless, we're going to have to leave. We're going to have to leave soon. The only thing I don't know how to do is get to the realm."

"I know how," Shade replied nervously. "There's only one entrance to that realm. You can't enter it from the portal. You can exit it from the portal, but the only way in is through the mountains. If we are going to go, we have to go soon."

"How are we going to get there?" Hobbles asked. "When you say the mountains, I'm assuming you don't mean in this realm. I'm assuming you mean the realm of the trolls. They don't have public transportation."

Shade looked perplexed. "I don't know, but hopefully, one of them will give us a ride on their backs, or maybe they've come forward in technology. Either way, it doesn't matter. We have to get there."

One of the elder witches standing close by cleared her throat. We glanced over at her, and she reached down, picking up her broom that she was using to sweep the floor with. She handed it over to Shade. "No better way to travel when there are many other options."

I gasped and pointed at the broom, slugging Shade in the arm. He winced and took the broom from the older woman. "Okay, okay. You got me. We ride on broomsticks sometimes."

"Ha! I knew it. You doing that here? In this realm?"

Shade rubbed his hand on his face. "I'll make you a deal. I'll tell you all about broomsticks, if we make a plan first. My brother's stuck in a realm that, with every moment that passes, he becomes like them. Admitting my broomstick is worth saving his life."

I patted him on the shoulder. "Well, I'm sorry it came to that, but I'm glad you've come to terms with it. I'm excited to ride on the back of your broomstick."

I couldn't even say that without giggling. Shade rolled his eyes and walked ahead of me, going back into the house. Willa smiled nervously and waited for the others to walk away. "Anything about my father?"

My face sank, and I didn't even think about asking the banshee when I was in her world. "Not yet. But the banshee said that the Witch King still played a big part, so hopefully, he has the answers about where we can find him. Come on, let's go get ready."

She reached out and grabbed my arm before I could walk away. "Unfortunately, I don't think I can come on this adventure. The Fae are very sensitive to the powers of the lost realm. I wouldn't make it more than a couple days in there before becoming part of their lost souls. But Hobbles and Shade should be able to get you there safely. I'll be waiting nervously here."

I was scared. Not having Willa with me was not something I thought I would ever have to face. No matter how strong the powers got, I was still unsure about myself and magic in general. Willa could tell my anxiety was rising, and she put her hand on my shoulder. I felt the spark of her magic, but unlike the years past when she would instantly calm me, it didn't work. She looked at her hand and placed it back in front of her, realizing that my powers had overridden hers. She leaned up and kissed me on the cheek. "I believe in you. I will take care of the people here, and you get their leader back."

I reached out and touched her shoulder. "And then we find your father, and we kick the shit out of the King Collector."

Willa laughed. "Damn right."

As I turned to go into the house, ready to gather my things, the smile on my face fell. Willa might've been sure of my abilities, but I wasn't. And if I went to the lost realm and couldn't save the Witch King, I wasn't sure I would be able to save myself either. A lot of things were riding on abilities that I didn't even know existed a few months before. Hopefully, he returned, but if I didn't, Willa would be on her own, and the fate of the realms would be doomed.

You know, no pressure at all.

COMING NEXT BOOK 4!

Loving the Story? Coming Soon, Book 4
Bye Bye Banshees
Join the Notification List

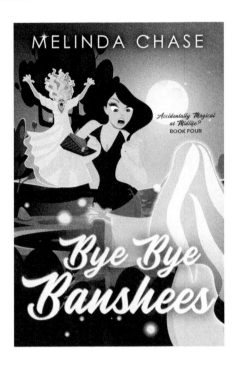

THANK YOU FOR READING!

It's always terrifying to release a book into the world. You don't know whether people will love it or hate it, but either way, you at least hope they *read* it.

Thank you so much for taking a chance on this author and grabbing my new series **Accidentally Magical at Midlife?**

This series is planned for 8 books, so make sure you've signed up for my newsletter to be notified of releases!

Also, I'm hard at work the next books at present. I can't wait to share them with you!

- Mel

WANT A FREE BOOK?

Join Melinda's Newsletter and Claim Your
Freebie!
Potions and Pearls

ALSO BY MELINDA CHASE

Midlife Mayhem Series

1. *Forty, Fabulous and . . . Fae?*

2. *Divorce, Divination and . . . Destiny?*

3. *Spandex, Spells and . . . Shadows?*

4. *Paranoia, Pixies and . . . Prophecies?*

5. *Heels, Hexes and . . . Heirlooms?*

6. *Truths, Tricks and . . . Traitors?*

7. *Myths, Mysteries and . . . Monsters?*

8. *TBA*

Accidentally Magical at Midlife?

1. *Gone with The Witches*

2. *Some Like it Hexed*

3. *Gentlemen Prefer Broomsticks*

4. *Bye Bye Banshees Coming July 2021*

5. *TBA - Coming August 2021*

6. *TBA*

I

FREE PREVIEW: FORTY, FABULOUS AND...FAE?

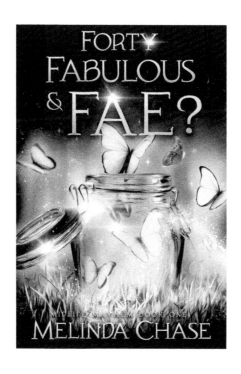

MIDLIFE MAYHEM BOOK ONE

No one expects their happily-ever-after to end at forty—but here I am one Prince Charming short of a fairytale.

Living back at Mom's place with her and Gram is not how this ex district attorney intended to start the next chapter of her life, but I shouldn't be surprised it's where I ended up.

You see, my family is cursed. *Literally.*

At least that's what both Gram and Mom claim. I've never given much thought to their ridiculous superstitions, but when three local patrons from my mom's occult shop end up dead, even I'm a bit unnerved.

So, I decide to dive right into the crazy headfirst. And what I thought would be the end of my journey...may only be the beginning.

1

"TAKE THE STUPID SHOES!" I screeched, while simultaneously launching my hardly worn pair of Louboutin's straight at my husband's head.

Ex-husband. I needed to start remembering that tiny, yet very significant detail.

To my absolute horror, Kenneth managed to duck, and narrowly avoided getting stabbed in the eye with the very sharp, stupidly irresponsible, and impossible to wear heel.

If only I had learned to throw when I was a child. Maybe that moment would have turned out differently.

But I guess I should back up a little bit.

My name is Shannon McCarthy. A boring name for a boring woman. And even more boring? Here I am, barely forty, the victim of a male midlife crisis, newly divorced, and forced to move back home to Portland, Oregon. Well, not forced. But right now, Portland seemed like a much better choice than Boston, where news of my husband's affair still littered the front pages of our local newspaper.

Who would have thought my life would turn out like this?

Not me, that's for damn sure. When I married Kenneth, with his smooth tan skin and devilish good looks, I really thought that was it for me. This was the guy I'd spend the rest of my life with. We'd have two very high profile careers, me as a D.A., and him as a judge, live in a big fancy house with a purebred Golden Retriever who listened to our every single command, and drive shiny new sports cars, like a Lamborghini, to and from our high-paying jobs every day. It was the life every single Boston girl dreams of.

And apparently, it was a life I no longer got to have. Not since Kenneth decided his pretty, young clerk was the place he should stick his junk, instead of being a respectable man and coming home to his wife.

So, here we were. I was in the middle of packing up the home we'd bought ten years ago, the one we were supposed to grow old in, while Kenneth sat on his butt and complained about every single thing I tried to box up. Anything he had bought me during the fifteen years we'd been married was apparently just a reminder of how much he had "given" me over the years.

As if I hadn't given him anything, too. I was the one who'd worked my tiny little butt off to put him through law school when I was on a public defender's salary, saving and pinching every penny I possibly could so that we didn't go hungry while he attended Northeastern.

"I should have sent you to Suffolk," I growled at him. "At least then, I wouldn't have wasted a hundred grand so you could be a corrupt judge."

"I am not a corrupt judge!" Kenneth hollered. "What part of this don't you get?"

"All of it!" I shrieked. "How could you throw away fifteen years of marriage for a fling? Fifteen years, Kenneth! We were building a life together. We were supposed to have—"

"Have what, Shannon?" he demanded, stepping up into my personal space. Those deep brown eyes of his bore into my green ones with a fury I'd only seen him use on the worst criminals, the ones he absolutely loathed and could never be impartial to.

I guessed I fell into that category now. The category of "People Kenneth Loathes."

"Have… it!" I sputtered as I attempted to articulate just what "it" was. But I couldn't find the words. "It" was huge. "It" encompassed so much that I couldn't possibly do it justice with a few shouted sentences.

"Yeah," Kenneth sneered. "'It' being the fancy house, the nice car, the dog."

Kenneth pointed an accusatory finger at Marley, our mutt. We weren't exactly able to spring for the Golden Retriever six years before.

"What's wrong with that?" I demanded. "I wanted a nice life, a comfortable one. I wanted to be happy in my marriage, unlike every other woman in my family. Is that too much to ask?"

Kenneth stopped. A brief flash of humanity leapt into his eyes, but then it was gone just as quickly. I almost wasn't sure if it had actually been there in the first place.

"Maybe it is," he finally whispered, his eyes downcast. "Because by asking for it, you tried to mold me into something I'm not… Something I could never be for you."

"All I asked was for you to love me," I murmured. Tears pricked my eyes, and I felt the brick wall I'd so carefully built in the last two weeks start to crumble and fall.

"No, you didn't." He shook his head and adjusted his navy blue tie. "You asked me to be this monument of a husband—like I was some character in a storybook. This isn't a story, Shan."

"It's our story," I insisted. I stepped up to him and cupped his soft, warm cheeks in my hands the way I always used to, begging him to look up at me.

To love me.

But he didn't. Kenneth leaned into my touch one last time before he shoved my hands off of him and stepped back, teary eyed.

"It's your story," he replied. "I have to go live my own story. And you're just not in it. I'm sorry. Really."

And I could see that he was. He thought that his apology was enough to make me forget that after fifteen years, he'd come home one night and just asked me for a divorce. Just like that. No nonsense, no lead in.

Kenneth started to walk down the giant, carpeted staircase, making a beeline for the door. I did my best to force myself to stay put. I couldn't watch him leave this time.

But my feet had other plans. Before I knew it, I was out of our enormous master bedroom and pressed up against the railing of our second floor landing.

"Ken?" I called out, right as his hand went to open our massive oak front door.

He froze, hand in the air, and didn't turn back to me.

"What?"

"Why her?" I couldn't help it. I needed to know what was so much better about this other woman. What made her worthy of breaking up a marriage?

Kenneth sucked in a huge breath, and then sighed. He didn't turn to look back at me when he spoke. I wasn't sure if it was because he couldn't bear to see the look on my face, or if he didn't want me to see the look on his.

"She and I want to live the same story, Shannon."

With that, the door slammed shut with a sound of such finality, I swear it could have happened in a Hitchcock movie.

The scream that ripped from my throat was so feral and animalistic, it almost sounded like a banshee. Not that I believed in those sorts of things.

When all of the sound had made its way out of me, and my vocal chords had been just about rubbed dry, I slowly turned back to the bedroom, where I had about fifteen boxes full of clothes to seal and pack.

Except they were all done.

Every single box that I had packed up was closed and sealed nicely with two layers of tape, as if some invisible assistant had come along and finished the task for me in mere moments.

For a second, my heart stopped, and my heavy panting caught in my throat.

"You're imagining things, Shannon," I muttered to myself. "You must have closed those boxes already."

But how could I have? The last thing I remembered doing was yanking a Louboutin out of an open box to throw at Kenneth. Even the box of shoes, though, was closed and sealed.

Freaked out, I headed down to the kitchen to finish packing. The movers would be coming in the morning, and I'd be on a flight home the next afternoon.

Home.

I hadn't been there for more than a brief, two-day visit in nearly ten years. It wasn't that I didn't love my mom and my Grams, or Grams' best friend, Dina. I loved them more than words could say.

It was their beliefs I didn't love. All three of them were impossibly superstitious, and whenever I was around, I always felt like there was some big secret I was missing out on, some sort of major thing I just didn't know.

Which was crazy. They were my family, and I knew everything there was to know about them all.

But still. My intuition always went haywire whenever I was in that house, the same one Mom had grown up in after her father had abandoned them.

The same one I'd grown up in.

Less than twenty-four hours after my final fight with Kenneth, I was in an Uber and on my way to the airport.

And stuck in traffic.

"Are you sure there are no backroads you can take to get us there faster?" I asked the driver, a stout young man with fire engine red hair, the same color as mine. He had a South Boston accent, and drove with his golfing hat on backwards.

"No, lady, sorry," the guy shrugged. "Traffic's real bad out today, huh?"

"Sure is," I sighed, and looked at my watch for the fifth time in as many minutes.

I had half an hour before the gates closed, I missed my flight, and I was stuck in Boston for... who knew how long. I just needed to get out, to go home and see my family and make some sort of attempt to reconnect with life itself. Figure out my next act.

Without Kenneth.

The traffic didn't improve, even by a smidgeon. I was late to the airport, and by the time I made it through security, I was sweaty and anxious as I sprinted through the terminal.

Just as I got up to my gate, I saw those big white doors start to close.

"No, wait!" I screamed, so loudly I turned a plethora of heads. The attendant either didn't hear me or didn't care, because those doors closed all the same.

"I... have... a ticket... for this flight," I gasped at the cranky old flight attendant manning the door. "I need to get on."

She looked up, appraised me with dark hazel eyes, and then shook her head with absolutely no remorse.

"Sorry," she shrugged. "Can't help ya. Get here earlier next time, like everyone else."

"No, look, you don't understand," I wailed. I could already feel it all coming down on top of me, revving up for a massive breakdown. The cheating, the divorce, the move, the pre-mid-life crisis I was about to have. "I'm getting a divorce, okay? Because my cheating ex-husband has some grand idea that he's going to go live a story, whatever that means. But he's not just living a story. Oh, no. He is living it with *someone else.* The man cheated on me and then had the gall to blame it on this insane need to 'live my own story.' What does that even mean? Do you know? Because I don't. I just... don't. So anyways, now I'm here, trying to get on this flight to go home and see my Mom and my Grams—who I haven't seen since Christmas, mind you. I am a terrible daughter, I know, save it. My ex used to tell me that all the time. He also said I was a terrible spouse, but he's the one who cheated, so you tell me who got the last word there, okay? All I'm really saying is that I need, and I mean *need*, to get on this flight and get the hell out of this city before the whole thing falls down and suffocates me. So is that too much to ask, for you to open those doors and let me get on my flight so I don't suffocate?"

Yeah.

It wasn't until after I'd finished, and felt that sort of out of breath panic a person feels after they've acted like a total idiot, that I realized I'd pretty much just dumped my entire life story on a total stranger.

And an entire airport terminal.

The stewardess, though, looked wholly unimpressed and unamused with my story. She just shook her head and sighed.

"Go back to customer service and they'll get you on the next flight," she informed me. "Have a good day."

She glanced back down at whatever stupid paper was on her desk, and that was when I lost it.

"Listen to me!" I hissed, crouching down so I could meet her eyes head on. "You need to let me on that flight. Now."

All of a sudden, the woman's hazel eyes went blank, kind of like a person's does in an over-acted TV scene where they're supposed to be hypnotized. She stared at me, and this scary smile twitched the corner of her lips, but didn't go all the way, and sure as hell didn't meet her eyes.

"Okay, you can get on this flight," she said

robotically, and then went to open the doors as if she was a puppet on a string.

I didn't even have time to question the strange oddity. I just nodded my thanks and rushed past her to get on that plane.

Keep Reading
Grab Your Copy Here!

ABOUT THE AUTHOR

Melinda Chase is an author of Paranormal Women's Fiction.

Over forty years young, Melinda loves writing tales that prove life—romance—and 'happily-ever-afters'—*do exist* beyond your twenties!

Her debut Series, *Midlife Mayhem* is a snarky, hilarious, romantic adventure, sure to please fans of traditional paranormal romance and cozy paranormal mysteries!

Join Her Newsletter Here!

Printed in Great Britain
by Amazon